Life Is a Strange Brew

Family Remembrances

Joanne Aber, Ph.D.

Dear Joan & Bill - I hope you enjoy the "plug" for the Angelo Gazebo Park. Thank you for your help with this book, Joanne

PUBLISH AMERICA

PublishAmerica
Baltimore

First printing

ISBN: 1-4137-2893-6
PUBLISHED BY PUBLISHAMERICA, LLLP
www.publishamerica.com
Baltimore

Printed in the United States of America

Another book by Joanne Aber:

Getting a College Degree Fast (1996)

Dedication

To my husband, Bill, the "wind beneath my wings;" and to our children, Daelyne and Erik, who have helped me see that life is to be lived with gusto. To the memory of my parents, Vera and David Aber, who were ahead of their time. To the memory of my mother- and father-in-law, Nancy and Basil Leschuk, who showed me their special caring. To the memory of Regina "Jene" Zuefle, who helped me see that a woman's dreams do come true.

To my family, Caryl, Rich, Julie, Lori and Lisa; to my friends who are family, Marj and Lee, Ron, Debbie, Judy, Tiya, Su-Su, Medora, Muriel, Lee and Chet; and to my church families at Pilgrim Congregational Church, First Church of Evans, Faith Christian Church and the ladies prayer group at New Life Christian Church. This book would have pages and pages of many more names space permitting; to all those who are family and friends who know how special each of you are to me in the tapestry of my life.

Acknowledgments

To the PublishAmerica staff for all their invaluable and sensitive help in getting this book to press; to Leda Johnson Ansbro, lifelong friend since our days at Eden Central High School, librarian, storyteller, and editor; to Juanita Busch Gibson for her help with this book and with life; and to Leslie Duncan Neilson, friend and fellow writer who encouraged me to publish this book. A special thank you to Caryl Aber McCaffrey, Joan Lemmler Will, Betty Ann Argauer O'Donnell, Anthony J. Cooper, Jr. and William and Joan Houston for their input on the finer details of these stories.

Note to My Readers...

Timeless

As we look deeply within,
We understand our perfect balance.
There is no fear of the cycles of life.
For when you stand in the moment,
You are timeless.

Robert Yee

Over the years my family and friends are woven closely into the tapestry of my life. Each has had loving, humorous and poignant impact on me. When a family story comes to mind, it is told over and over. These stories are enjoyed with each telling as if it was the first time. Each is a cherished, heartfelt moment in time.

My writing is conversational for the most part. With this in mind, please enjoy the sentiments, the wondrous adventures and yes, even some of life's sadness. As I wrote these stories for my family about my family and friends, some have been published in bits and pieces elsewhere. Each time my "fan" mail would tell me that my stories brought back family and childhood memories to my readers.

After reading many of these stories, Isla, one of the dearest ladies I know said, "I feel like I am right there when I read one of your stories."

Juanita, another dear friend said, "This is a wrap yourself in a blanket on a rainy day by a cozy fire with a cup of hot chocolate book."

Tony, one of my friends from my hometown said, "The walk down Main Street in "My Hometown," brought back many special memories of my family."

With that high praise, I give you my book and one of my favorite sayings...

> I am not afraid of tomorrow, for I have seen yesterday, and love today.
>
> W. A. White (found in our son Erik's high school graduation program)

Walk in sunshine,

Joanne Aber, Ph.D.
Wichita, Kansas and Derby,
New York and all points between

My Mother

Vera Hamscher Aber was my mother. She had what I always called her "Mona Lisa" smile and a contagious laugh. She was a daughter, sister, aunt, cousin and friend to so many people before she married. She married at thirty-one, was a mother for the first time at thirty-five and a grandmother at fifty-nine.

In the 1930s and 40s, it would be fair to say she was a late bloomer in the traditional roles of her life. In her nursing career and many social ways, she was not only ahead of her time, she was a liberated woman.

She was raised Protestant, the middle child of nine, eight sisters and one brother, by a knowing mother and father. Most of her savvy in life seemed to come from an inner common sense and a personal spirituality, not necessarily from formal education and religion.

Mom's graduation from high school was in part because her father died young, when my mother was barely a teenager. Mom always said as sad as that was for her family, had her dad lived she and her younger sisters would not have gone on in school. My grandfather only let her older sisters complete the eighth grade.

When my Gramma Louisa was widowed, she worked from her home and supported her minor children as a clever business woman without a formal education. Because of this, she insisted all the girls at least graduate from high school. Mom wanted to be a registered nurse, which her mother encouraged.

Since my mother was single longer than her sisters, she pursued her dream of becoming a registered nurse. She worked in nursing all her life all her life even with a family and part-time after she retired. This was a godsend for our family because my father experienced many years of unemployment based on ageism.

Mom's many talents included her German English American gourmet cooking, crochet and knitting, gardening, bird watching and photography. And, her green thumb gardening fed her soul. The fruits of her floral displays and landscaped groupings delighted those who passed by our house, or sat in our yard among her gardens.

When she worked in her gardens, she would hum or sing her favorite Gershwin and Broadway tunes like "A Pretty Girl Is Like a Melody," and "Someone to Watch Over Me." Or sing one of her favorite hymns, "In the Garden" and "Morning Has Broken."

Bird watching was another of her nice weather pasttimes. Although, she made sure her feathered friends had suet feeders around our yard in the wintertime.

She had bird books and a pair of old mother-of-pearl opera glasses sitting on the sill of our living room picture window. She watched them wherever they were as they flew around and landed here and there in her adjacent gardens. As well as when they fed at the bird feeders, or went in and out of the bird houses she had place around our yard.

She and many of her nurse friends had bird pictures on their stationery and Christmas cards. They were that taken with birds.

My parents...

No story about my Mom would be complete without my Dad. They were soul mates. Each was very unique in his or her own way. That is what led them to each other, and to become our parents. They went together for several years. Dad was thirty-six when they eloped on Christmas Eve, 1941.

When they would tell the story of how they had eloped, Dad always told how Mom was a half hour late for their wedding. He thought she stood him up. Not intentional, but it was due to the snow and ice on the Buffalo streets.

Each of them had many family sayings. One of Mom's when she was upset, "I have a mind to do this or say that."

Half a mind? Where did she get that? We don't recall anyone in her family saying that.

Another favorite, whenever an affluent person would complain about their tough times, she would say, "If I had their money, I'd burn mine."

Dad was an armchair storyteller and his favorite sayings seemed to come from his stories. He told us about his family adventures before during and after they migrated from Easton, Pennsylvania through Akron, Ohio and settled in Buffalo. And so it was that many of his sayings came from his rural heritage as he spun his stories.

When Dad thought we needed a haircut, he would

say, "You look like a boonder, it's time to have your mother cut your hair."

What is a boonder? No one I have ever talked to seems to know, not even those who are from his hometown area. Since he was a very creative thinker, he might have originated it himself.

Among their many joint country living endeavors, Mom and Dad had a three- to four-acre vegetable garden with grapevines. It was legendary among our family, friends and town's people. Many sat around our table and enjoyed home-grown food that Mom prepared in unusual ways. These foods did not just stay at our table, Mom took them to family reunions, a friend's home or a community's covered dish supper.

Neither Mom nor Dad ever met a stranger...

Dad was a people person in public but more of a loner in private. He saw the value of Dr. Norman Vincent Peale's philosophy of positive thinking. He was a political commentator and thought along the lines of today's pithy talk show hosts. At times he became overbearing with his take on politicians.

People shunned him when he was like this. Oddly, some of what he said was in line with the eventual events of Watergate. He had Alzhiemers in his 60s and 70s and most of his family and friends had passed by the time he died at eighty-one.

Both of my parents read the early materials on vitamins and herbs. Dad was for them; Mom, being traditionally trained in medicine, was more cautious. Eventually she took some vitamins and herbs in her senior years.

In the 1950s, both of them refused to let us be part of

the polio vaccine tests. I was twenty before I had my first oral polio vaccine. Although we did have the routine vaccinations required to attend school.

All to many times, Dad was a person of no influence with his community even though he was highly intelligent and had uncanny awareness. His take on nutrition, and supplements and herbs was that they were the answer to prevention and cures to all our illnesses, even cancer. But like his unsolicited political pronouncements, not everyone wanted to hear what he was trying to share with them.

Mom was a people person in pubic and private. She was known and loved by our community for herself and her volunteer work as a nurse. She shared many of Dad's opinions, but did not talk openly about them. To this day, when I have lived in our hometown for a few years at a time or visit, people who knew my mother come up to me and tell me a heartfelt memory of what a good friend and person she was. Or that she helped them when they needed it and many times it was just between them

In her late 60s and through her 70s until she passed at seventy-six, Mom had suffered from the debilitating effects of diabetes and near blindness. In addition to a large number of family and friends at her memorial, I received many cards. Some added notes of their special memories of my mother. These remembrances brought sentimental tears and do to this day.

They were all special uplifting memories to us. But one of the sweetest was sent to me from a longtime childhood friend. I had never met her but knew of her and saw her pictures and her family's pictures that she shared with Mom in letters and annual Christmas cards.

She wrote that when her father died, it meant her mother had to work. They moved to our road to live with her maternal grandparents. They cared for her while her mother worked.

She felt the loss of her father, her home, her friends and even her mother to some extent. Then, she had to live in a place she only visited for holidays and country visits. She was undone.

Until there was a knock at the door. The ten-year-old girl standing there said, "Hello, my name is Vera."

They were dear friends from that moment on.

The stories in this book are from the happy-go-lucky country days of Mom's youth, her early career, early married years through to my early teens. Some parts of these stories even take me to Mom's middle age and later years in her life. Dad is in these family stories from the time when he met and married my mother and on through my early teens.

This book is written about family including my dad, my sister, close family friends and me. The heart of it is my mom.

Vera and David Aber's silhouette self-portrait circa 1943.

Table of Contents

My Mother 11

Our Family's Early Years 19

- My Hometown 21
- Our Tarpaper House 44
- Country Living 55
- The Toaster 64
- Summer Cottages 86
- My Two Grammas 95
- My Aunt's Dishes and My Uncle's Plums 102

Adventures 111

- Mom's Chickens, Cow and Ducks 113
- Childhood Antics 116
- Kindergarten 119
- Wintry Days 123
- The Sandwich Under The Car 126
- Our Family Road Trip 129
- The Lake Effect 136

Special Times 139

- Lazy Hazy Days of Summer 141
- Bible School and the Palomino Horse 144
- Hiding Out in the Choir 147
- The Violin 150
- The Hawthorn Tree 152
- Mom's Barley Soup 154

Celebrations 157

Birthday Parties 159
Easter Time 162
Halloween of Days Gone By 165
Grampa's Christmas Desk 168
Mom's Christmas Gifts 172

Our Family's Early Years

A family, however defined, is where we all come from. It is a treasured gift we have from our birth through our life's journey to our passing.

My Hometown

Our Tarpaper House

Country Living—Marshmallows, Pets, a Stone Fireplace, the Sulfur Pump and Water Pails, and My Sister in the Corner

The Toaster—Tonsils, the Kitchen Cabinet, Bee Stings and Childhood Accidents

Summer Cottages—Grandparents, Parents, Aunts, Uncles and Cousins, Strawberries and the Country Store

My Two Grammas—Gramma Louisa and Gramma Edith

My Aunt's Dishes and My Uncles Plums—Land, Trees, White Bibles and Antiques

My Hometown

My hometown was and still is special. But first, I want to tell about the road where we lived and our house and our neighborhood.

In the early 1900s, my mother's family was from Buffalo, New York. My grandfather and great-uncle decided to move their families to the country. At first, they owned land in Hamburg south of Buffalo. But they did not move there.

This was the town where the word hamburger was coined at the 1885 Hamburg Expo. It was a simple food item—a beef burger served on a hard roll. As its popularity grew the bun evolved to the softer rolls we now call hamburger buns.

Hamburg was rural then, but had a village with the potential to become a small city. Both families wanted to be out in the boonies, away from any business districts. They wanted an area that would be rural with farming potential for twenty-five years or longer. With that in mind, they traded their land with a man who owned a mile of land on either side of Burns Road, Derby. As an added value our road was about six miles from Lake Erie's sandy beaches even though the area was farmland with wooded lands between grids.

My grandfather chose a parcel of land he owned and built a large farmhouse on the hill of the property. Then he moved his family to the country. My mother was ten, and she and her older teenage sisters and their one brother finished growing up there. Eventually our house was on the property next to it. The two properties were separated by unusual woods.

Please, read more about this woods a bit later, and in "Country Living," and "Summer Cottages."

Soon after my mother's family moved to the country, my grandfather and great-uncle kept other parcels of land they wanted, then they sold the other land. They sold it to relatives, relatives of relatives, and friends of relatives.

Later in their years on Burns Road, my grandfather built my grandmother a dream house that was more like a city home. By this time he was a traveling salesman. Still he built a big barn behind it but it was sided like the house. He was not going to give up his farming. It was and remains one of the nicest, Cape Cod style houses there.

Shortly after he finished that house and they were in it nearly two years, he died in a one-car train collision. Many years earlier he had bought an insurance policy that gave my grandmother $40 a month as long as she had minor children at home. This was something that was seldom done in those days.

Part of Gramma's survival meant she and her children raised produce for sale and their use. This meant she and the minor children could live in their new home for a few years after Grampa died. To continue to make ends meet she finally sold their seasonal delicacy of baby limas to the Statler Hotel dining room in the city.

When most of her children were raised, Gramma sold her dream house and moved to the city. The buyer was a relative of a relative from the city. And, according to my mother, this family did not fully pay Gramma for her house. That aside, my youngest three aunts finished growing up in the city and graduated from city high schools.

As a postscript, my great-uncle never did move his family to our road. He decided he was in it for the land speculation and profit. As each of my older aunts and uncle reached twenty-one, my grandparents offered each of them a parcel of land. Three of them accepted, my mother among them.

Our neighborhood...

To this day, as you drive down our road to our neighborhood, as when my grandparents first did, you will encounter a unique railroad bridge. It has been serving the New York highway and national railroad transportation systems for nearly one hundred years.

This railroad bridge is the landmark at the beginning of the parcels of land my grandfather and my great-uncle owned. It is built into the side of a hill at an angle. Now days it takes driving agility to go through it one car at a time. Back when it was new, it took agility to drive a horse drawn buggy, sleigh, work wagon, horseless carriage, or a Model T through it as well.

At first, most who bought land from our family built cottages to be out in the cooler country and near the beaches. Eventually the cottages became year-round homes. Even at that, all looked like cottages until further additions and winterizing happened, except the one that belonged to my second cousins. Outwardly it looked like a complete two-story house.

Please, read more about this cottage in "Our Tarpaper House" and "Summer Cottages."

It was a fairly close-knit neighborhood. We all knew

the year-round and summer families who lived on our road and one connected road. Between World Wars I and II, the cottage owners continued to enjoy the country from the end of June until Labor Day, especially on the weekends. By the late 1940s, the cottages began to have full-time families living in them. By 1950, many of the converted cottages were sold to new owners. After that time, all new buildings were family homes, not cottages.

Next to our land was a small a wedge of land my younger aunt owned. It was vacant. It had a small crater hole in among the trees that my mother told us had been the dirt basement under a house. Around 1920, it burned to the ground and was not rebuilt.

My aunt who owned it did not mind that we used part of it for our yard and activities. Our lawn expanded over the years onto my aunt's land. We enjoyed my aunt's Blue Spruce trees at the edge of our lawn area. The wind originally brought them to that spot. The Spruces were at the beginning of the thicket and woods. At the edge of this cleared area we had a rope swing hung between two of the giant Oak trees just past the Spruces.

Each summer, the area behind the swing had an acre of black berry bushes hanging heavy with berries. We sat by them and just ate the berries off the bush and watched the clouds roll by. Mom made jams and pies from them.

The next parcel of land past my younger aunt's belonged to second oldest aunts. My older aunt's land was deeper in acreage, as was ours, and went back to the big woods that crossed the property parcels on this section of our road.

Please, read more about the big woods in "Our Tarpaper House," "Country Living," "Summer Cottages," and later in this story.

My older aunt never really used her land. As it turned out, the father of the boy down the road worked a usage deal with my aunt. He housed his chicken coops with chicken wire fences and farmed the land behind them up to the edge of the big woods. Some years after he started his gentleman farmer work, he planted acres of Christmas trees on acreage the was alongside of our land and to the side of the land where he raised produce. After years of use, he bought the land from my aunt.

Woods, woods, woods...

When you arrived at our house, you would see our lawn was between two woods. One was next to a small creek and was an unusual woods. It was, and continues to be, like no other we have seen.

The trees are soft maple and the ground is covered with a floor of Myrtle. Due to the shade and the soil content, it has aqua-hazed colored leaves rather than the usual dark green of most Myrtle. It is breathtaking to see violet blooms over the aqua. And, here and there are Blue Bells and Star-of-David. During the summer months deep in the middle there are some Jack-in-the Pulpits. On the edges, spring through fall, there are sun-kissed ferns galore.

In the late 1920s, when one of my third oldest aunt was a teenager, she worked as a house helper at local estates. Myrtle was everywhere. She brought home a few clumps of it. My grandmother and aunt planted them at the top of the hill at the edge of our woods on the side near their house. Over the years this Myrtle grew downhill completely covering the woods' floor.

Whenever my aunt took credit for this ground cover, my mother would smile her "cat that swallowed the mouse smile." Some years later, I commented on the phenomenal growth of Myrtle from a few clumps planted those years ago. Mom finally told me the secret of our woods.

While it was true that my aunt had started the Myrtle, unbeknownst to the family my mother would add new clumps of Myrtle from friends' gardens. And, she kept moving some of the plants from all the clumps around to get it evenly distributed as it is today. Mom let her sister have the credit since she did start the Myrtle and because that was how her family was.

Please, read more about my mother's green thumb efforts in "The Hawthorn Tree" and "Easter Time."

The late 1930s, the 1940s and early 1950s...

A few years after my mother graduated from nursing school, she was head nurse at the Juliette Goodyear Home for Children on the northern edge of the city. She lived there during the week, but on weekends wanted to be out in the country. Being nearly thirty with a well paid job, she had a cottage built at the top of the hill on her land. It was her weekend place in her beloved woods.

Over the years after my parents were married and lived there, they cleared trees out of their land to make a yard with a lawn. But they left the majority of all the woods on both sides in tact as well as the small woods behind their chicken coops at the back edge of the yard near our house.

Please, read more about this in "Mom's Chickens, Cow and Ducks."

Of our front two woods, we played the most in our special woods. The third woods, I just mentioned was between our house just before the open fields at the back part of our property. That woods was just there, but not one we played in because it had some wet lands where an underground stream surfaced and ran into the creek that ran alongside our property.

There was a fourth woods that you will read about later. This was part of a large-treed area that went across all the land at the end of all the adjoining surveyed properties. As you will read, all of our woods were wonderful places.

Please, read more about the big woods in "Country Living," "The Toaster," and "Summer Cottages."

My hometown...

Before I take you to Main Street, Angola, I need to tell you about the composition of my hometown. It is the combination of two towns together, Derby and Angola. Derby was more rural with a post office and a few churches, and businesses. But it did not have a cohesive business district other than Highland. It had a small plaza area, with a large locally-owned drug store, some gas stations, a barber and beauty shop, and a few restaurants and taverns. But those businesses were separated then, and now, by a main highway, making that business district less cozy, not a walk-around.

In the 70s, Highland became more of a business district surrounded by several new housing developments. This gave Derby, the township Highland was in, a serious business district with a new modern plaza with a major supermarket and drug store chain added to our independently owned drug store, even a Radio Shack and a discount store. Nationally known fast food restaurants popped up including McDonald's, Burger King, and Pizza Hut.

Just before and during the arrival of these chains, the business district grew as independent business were added like an optical shop, a car wash, a donut shop a few locally owned modern restaurants, two laundry mats, and more beauty and barber shops. Even a full service bait shop came about to accommodate the new marina a few miles away. But even now, as back then, a car is needed to shop in this business area.

The village...

The Village of Angola was, and remains, a village. There is a part of Angola, called the town that has the houses surrounding the village with an industrial park and major super market chains. And to add to the confusion, all these small towns and hamlets, including Derby, were incorporated into the Town of Evans. I have no idea where the name came from. It just is.

As I recall the Main Street of Angola, my memory is not all inclusive. What I remember are the business places where my family shopped or did business.

In the village, it was like the street and the people were embraced in one big hug. It was not a Utopia, but the warmth and caring that each person had for another was real and could be felt by all as they waved to each other as we walked the main street. Some of this was created by the closeness of the businesses. Once you parked your car, then and now, you could walk to do most of your shopping.

Yes, we were customers, so of course the business owners were friendly. It was more than that. The business owners and clerks considered their customers to be friends. There was no pressure to buy, no gimmickry signs, no bait and switches.

As you drove into Angola from the countryside there were *the* routes that the local people took. In the summertime this community hosted thousands from the city who came to the beaches on Lake Erie's shoreline, just a few miles from this business district. And they took the main routes into the village that were marked on road maps.

There is still a running debate if it is faster to turn and come out at the Y or drive straight and miss the Y. Oh, yes, these are the little things that make a place special to its longtime residents and a cherished memory to those of us who have our hometown remain in our hearts.

Dr. Cooper's Office...

The first place that I remember in the business district was Dr. Cooper's office. A small town doctor who took care of us by himself. No nurses, no receptionist, no computer billing clerk, and, for the most part, no third party pay.

His office was a cozy haven for the sick. And it was the front rooms of his house. His children were often heard running and playing and, yes, even yelling on the other side of the walls as we waited in his crowded waiting room. As they grew older, the doctor and his family moved to a large home that had been his wife's family home. This gave the children a country setting to run and play out of harm's way from the traffic of the village.

There were no appointments, first come first serve. If you wanted to be seen early during the office hours Tuesday through Friday from 2-4PM, you had to get there by noon and wait two hours. By the time the doctor came in and opened the door to his office, the seats were full and people were standing around the room. In nice weather, some waited outside, sitting on the cement steps.

He took cash mostly and checks if need be. This was before credit cards.

My mother and he were colleagues. We had limited credit at times on our medical bills. And I am sure we got a discount, one professional to another. But then, Dr. Cooper considered everyone in town family and extended a lot of credit. Seldom did he have to send a bill. People knew what they owed him and stopped by to pay him when they got the money, or paid him the next time they saw him for a medical reason.

What did those kids—eight boys and two girls who played on the other side of the wall while we waited to see their father—become when they grew up? No medical doctors, but they all got degrees: nine bachelor degrees, four master degrees, four doctorates and two nursing diplomas. The oldest son is a hospital administrator and the two JDs are each a town justice, one for our town and one for a neighboring town.

The New Angola Theater...

On down Main Street, next to the post office was the movie theater. It was *the* place to be on a Saturday afternoon. Mr. Geitner, the theater owner, had pictures of his favorite celebrities on the walls around the ticket window and behind and alongside the concession stand. They had posed with him when they were in Buffalo as part of their national tours promoting their latest movies.

He liked to talk about each one and it took very little encouragement. I remember one Saturday when we were about twelve, he talked to a few of us. He told us how nice Jane Powell was and how tiny.

The theater owner put a labor of love into his theater. It had elegant burgundy curtains and seats. It was always clean and the popcorn has never been as good as the popcorn in my memory from my hometown theater. And, the Milk Duds were fresh and melted in our mouths as good chocolate usually does. They were not stale like they are at most theaters now days.

In the mid-70s, it was still operational when my children were ten and five. We took them to the movies there and they enjoyed it. Coming from a bigger city to live in my hometown, they never expected such a posh theater in a small town to enjoy modern movies.

In the early 2000s, the theater was restored and opened. Our local non-profit group for the developmentally disabled adult residents work there. They are supervised ticket takers, concessionaires, ushers and the maintenance crew. All profits go to run the theater. And, I am told over 100,000 theater goers have viewed first run movies since the reopening.

The Angola 5 &10 Store...

This store had an ambiance like none other I have ever gone into before or since. It had wooden floors and was set up in a rather unusual way.

As you entered, there were shelves in front of you and back behind you up against the two big front windows that displayed merchandise to passers-by. As you walked to the left or right of the center island of shelves, you wove your way down the sides of the store to the back. The store had merchandise from shelves at waist level all the way up to the ceiling. The cash register was in the middle of the store between the two center islands of shelves.

The things you could find in this home-owned 5 &10 store seemed endless. As elementary children we bought our bulk valentines there.

The owner and the long-time clerks sold to several generations of children. As I reached my teens, the plazas had happened. Still, the merchandise was excellent and the prices competitive. And, like the other home-owned stores in the village, this small hometown store managed to stay in business until the 1990s, many, many years past the happening of local plazas and malls.

The Village Hall...

This building housed the police station, and offices for the Angola Village's mayor, clerk of the town, zoning, building inspectors, and registrar of deeds. To say it was provincial would be unfair. But to let you know how it was run would be the thing to do here.

This was a town that carried the political spoils system into the 1980s. When an election caused a change in the mayor's office, the majority party would replace all the clerks and village employees with those of their party. When the federal law changed the personnel took and passed their civil service tests to have their ratings. This was supposed to stop this kind of job termination. But the village continued to use the spoil system.

A lawsuit by the laid off workers followed and the village lost. It had to reinstate the former employees who lost their after an election. Their win meant the village had to pay all back pay and their court costs. It cost the town well over $100,000. But the village did learn compliance to a federal law.

The bowling alley...

Across from the Village Hall was the local bowling alley. For the 1950s and 60s, it was a stereotypical place with a tavern up front. It was an older crowd, mostly men, who just wanted to bowl and drink. Chicks was the newer bowling alley out in the township on the state highway. It had a bar uit the focus was a family restaurant and family bowling in the alleys which all made it more of a family place.

Lemmler's Shoe Store...

This shoe store is so real in my mind. My mother went from elementary through high school with the owner, his wife, and in-laws. We got our shoes there for years past the time the plazas had their glitzy shoe stores. The building was old and campy but the shoes were modern.

And, the truth be known, I am almost sure as I think back, my mother probably had a courtesy credit account there. Especially when it came time for school shoes or a special occasion.

Like the doctor's office, the movie theater and the 5 & 10, you felt like you were visiting a friend in Lemmler's shoe store. Even the clerks who worked for Mr. Lemmler treated the customers like family and friends. Both of the lady clerks were very attractively dressed and wore an appropriate amount of make-up for that day and time. They were very professional even though they were not in management. This was the same for the clerks who worked in the 5 & !0 Store and LaClair's.

The owner's daughter went on to be one of a group of the moving business forces behind the village's modernization over the years. She was a marketing director for the local bank and for its new branches. One year she was honored as Business Woman of the Year by the Evans Business and Professional Women's Club.

In recent years, she told me the store, Matteson's Shoe Store, was begun by her great-aunt and great-uncle. It was named after their last name. Of course, she was right. And, as the family story goes, her mother bought the store to keep it in the family while her father was serving in World War II. This was a gutsy thing for a woman with a small baby to do who was waiting for a husband who might not have come back from the war.

But by any other name, it will always be Lemmler's to me.

The Evans National Bank...

Again, this was a business that people knew who they were dealing with. To help the children, it offered a saving stamp program that came to our schools. We brought a quarter or quarters each week and bought red stamps to paste into a savings book. When the book was filled, we cashed it in for the paper money or began a savings account with the bank.

Christmas clubs were one of its top draws. You could get them from $25 to $500. They were not interest yielding accounts. Shrewd on the bank's part, if you saved weekly, at Christmas time you had cash to buy what you wanted. Still, to do this, you made a habit of going to the bank on a regular basis.

As late as 1971, my mother would buy a Christmas Club for her first grandchild. Up until then, she would buy them for us many years after we were married. It was her main gift to us for Christmas.

Shultz's Hardware Store...

This was locally owned and was a marvel, much like the 5 & 10. It had similar wooden floors. It, too, had shelves that went to the ceiling. But it had a second story with more hardware goodies than anyone could remember. It was a virtual handy man's paradise.

The fancier plaza stores opened but the local people were loyal to this unique hardware store. After we grew up and left home, my mother had priced law mowers. She had even priced them from our neighbor who had an Allis Chalmers dealership. But the Angola Hardware store sold her one she could afford and even arranged for payments with the local bank.

She had that lawn mower for over nearly twenty years, not one repair was ever needed. She took it to have the blade sharpened and a new spark plug every few years. But that was it. If memory serves, it was still running well when we sold her house many years later. And, Shultz's Hardware Store is open to this day over one hundred years after it first opened its doors.

La Clair's Clothing Store...

La Clair Miller's was the local women's and girls' dress store. Mr. La Clair was one of the owners and managed the store. I never met Mr. Miller. I suspect he was the original owner and Mr. La Clair and he worked together until Mr. La Clair bought him out. But the first owner's name was well known and the store kept the joint name, even after Mr. Miller was no longer part of it.

Besides up-to-date clothes for women and children, and some men's clothing, it had yard goods and sewing notions. The clothes in it were gorgeous, timely and reasonably priced. But the yard goods were outstanding.

When I was going to graduate from the sixth grade, it was the first place we shopped for my dress. But I was an in-between size. Hesitantly, my mother decided to try a dress shop she liked in Hamburg.

If I think hard enough, I can still smell the clean dye smells of new clothes in both stores as we entered. The Hamburg store was a bit pricier than LaClair's, but it was my graduation. She commented more than once that it would have been more "reasonably priced" if it had been at La Clair's.

Unfortunately for me, I was only five feet three inches tall and overweight. The only dress my mother found that fit, and could afford, was a light pink organdy dress. A dress that was made of beautiful material, but made me feel like I looked like a parade float.

Not by profession, but by avocation my mother was a custom seamstress. She always made our clothes for special occasions. I can only speculate that she did not have the time to make a dress and bought this one. But for the most part, if she did not make our clothes from materials at this store we bought them at La Clair's.

LaClairs did not close until the late 70s. This store is yet another testimony to the way businesses kept going regardless shift in shopping to the plazas and malls.

The Angola Pharmacy and Drug Store...

This small but efficient store was next to LaClair's. It had a card selection that would rival any mall store today albeit smaller in over all space. I remember it being in the center of the store as we walked in.

My mother told me that when we were adults, Dr. Cooper was a customer one day and he heard a woman in the card aisle laughing. He followed the laughing to find my sister reading the funny cards.

The A&P Grocery Store...

Across the railroad tracks from La Clair's and Shultz's Hardware Store and a bit set back behind the train depot was the first modern supermarket. The Angola A&P was a one stop grocery and meat shopping that included some pharmacy items but no prescription medicines.

The village had a local butcher shop. Oddly, the butcher shop was in business long after the A&P closed about ten years or so after it opened. A few year before it closed, a new supermarket chain opened out on the state highway on the edge of the town. This chain joined an already established supermarket out on the highway that has since been bought by two big food chains over the years while the first big food chain store to put A&P out of business has long since closed.

The butcher shop never really officially closed. The owner, I am told, chose to move to another small town some twenty miles away over a lease consideration. It is still there and selling choice meats as it did in our town regardless of the meat department of chain grocery stores.

The Angola Library...

We had school field trips to this library. The librarians were local women who our families knew. Each treated the children like we were relatives. It was a place you wanted to go even when school was not in session.

It was a very impressive place for the children of our town. My sister and I would check out library books on a weekly basis. We each had a limit of ten books as children. We would gather nearly twenty books each week and then have to wheedle the stack down to our ten. Then we would write a list of the books we had to leave behind for the next week. Of course, we did not read them all. Our eyes were big and we thought it was possible week after week. What did we know? We were children.

The Angola Train Depot...

Across from the merchants, but near the A&P, standing by itself was the train depot. It had long since stopped having regular passenger trains by the time I was five. But it had freight trains stop since we had some small industries, a canning factory and a brewery in full operation. At one time we had a full-scale bicycle factory.

The local schools would arrange for a passenger train coming through to Buffalo from Chicago, Cleveland, and Erie to stop and pick us up. We had the joy of a real train ride. Back then, it was thought that the passenger train would eventually become extinct. Our teachers wanted us to have this experience. Little did they, or anyone, envision AmTrak.

The feed store...

The south end of Main Street kitty corner across from the train station was a feed store. It was a wealth of supplies. Our town was on the edge of a rural farm community. My mother bought feed for her chickens there when she could not get to the larger coops. We got our bulk dog food when we had a dog. This was before Purina Dog food and some of the others made the bulk bags available at retail outlets.

Before we leave the village...

Whenever our parents would shop at the A&P Store or Shultz's Hardware Store we would browse in the 5&!0, cruise by La Clair's front windows or go to the library. In our youth we could walk this entire two blocks and back without our parents and be safe.

All our local stores had such an ambiance. It was an event to go to them even if we did not buy anything. As with all the merchants, we went to school with the owner's or manager's children. Many of the local ladies worked at these stores as clerks, some for years. One mother of a friend worked at Lemmler's and then the

A&P. Other mothers I knew worked at Lemmler's and the 5 &10. When La Clair's closed and the new discount stores came into the area, the clerks who worked there had so much retail experience they were hired as managers and assistant managers from the start.

The beach...

Evans Town Park was our little bit of paradise. It is not that much by today's standards or even back then, but it was perfect to us. And, you had to be a town resident to get in. And, we were.

To get to the beach there was, and still is, a tunnel under the road that went by the park. We loved to run through it, as did all the other kids, and yell at the top of our lungs to hear the echo.

We would run up the incline and past the open-roofed pavilion to the beach. As our feet hit the sand, we sunk in over our ankles. But we trudged through the sand. Throwing our towels down and kicking off our sandals, we ran into the water.

We knew our parents would lay their blanket down and watch our towels and sandals. We would look over our shoulders as we ran and see they were slowly walking down the sand to where our towels laid.

Then when they were in the water with us, we would ask them to watch our water stunts, or count as we tired to hold our breath under water. When our hour was up, we would drag ourselves out of the water.

We were warm in the water. But in between the water and the car we would shiver in the cool night air. Once in the car, we were surrounded by warmth. As we rode in the back seat, we were already thinking about the next night's beach time.

Please, read more about our beach time in "The Lake Effect."

The Tastee Freeze...

If you had a car, and who in a rural town or surrounding area did not, you drove to the local Tastee Freeze out on the state highway. The soft serve ice cream was worth the drive to dive into it face first. Hard scoop ice cream took a back seat to the Tastee Freeze ice cream and banana splits and other concoctions and cones dipped in hot chocolate that dried to a thin layer.

This Tastee Freeze had the Oaken Bucket. It was a combination of soft ice cream with ingredients similar to a banana split with more ice cream flavors, gobs of whip cream, pineapple and maraschino cherries and so much more.

Hard ice creams came back in over the years. Now days both soft and hard ice cream are served at the same places even the Tastee Freeze. But back then, the soft serve was the order of the day. On a hot summer's eve, after swimming in the lake at the town park, it was nirvana to wait for nearly a half hour in line to get one of these cool delights.

The Grandview Drive-In...

Behind the Tastee Freeze was the local drive-in. Our parents took us to see a movie or two. But our real time there was as teenagers, piled in a car, with some of us hiding in the trunk at times to save money to get in.

This drive-in was the first place we had delicious one or

two-person pizzas that were not made from scratch, as the pizzas were at local pizzerias. It was also the first place we had French Fries with vinegar. What taste delights. After that, I noticed that the hot dog stands in Western New York served them this way, and still do to this day.

The hot dog stands...

These were many, and still are, around our hometown area. They are close to the beach, but now days even the non-beach goers drive to them for that charcoal-grilled dog with everything on it and a side of fries that you drench in vinegar.

On a warm summer's evening in Western New York, there is nothing, absolutely nothing, like sitting at a hot dog stand biting into a New York hot dog. As it melts in your mouth, you savor the expansive view of the lake as a warm breeze washes over your face. And, you are surrounded by other lake people.

The Strawberry Festival...

Brant, the town known for its strawberry truck farms was next to our town. It had a strawberry festival that evolved to include a contest for the annual strawberry queen. A gal friend from school made it once as queen. And, my sister ran but did not get the crown. Before the days of sunscreen, she did get sunburned sitting in an evening gown on her float for the entire parade route. Nonetheless, it was a worthwhile experience.

The strawberries were the average size of a small peach or plum. We ate strawberries two and three times a day at the festival in some form or another—strawberry short cake, fresh strawberries, strawberry drinks.

The New Angola Gazebo Park...

Some of these businesses are still on Main Street, Angola, New York. Others are ghosts of the past in our town's history. In recent years, the town built a gazebo park behind the post office on Main Street on a side street between the business district and the residential area. Every Wednesday, all summer long, until Labor Day, they have outdoor concerts.

The concerts are such a draw that during each season some well-known celebrities come and sing for our town. They are usually there to do concerts in Buffalo or at our historically big Erie County Fair and Expo.

No admission. Bring a lawn chair or blanket to sit on. Popcorn and soft drinks sold for a modest price. The camaraderie of being with hometown folks is priceless.

Our Tarpaper House

Our house was covered with tarpaper for over ten years. Underneath the tarpaper was a finished house. It was sided with what was called novelty interwoven raised and lowered wooden siding. It was similar in design to vinyl siding of today.

Back then, if novelty siding was painted every five years or so, it was durable. If it was not painted, it would deteriorate in less than ten years. When that happened, no amount of painting would restore it. Usually, the siding would have to be totally replaced.

As our siding was nearing the five-year mark, Dad was not able to paint it. He wanted to protect it until he could paint the entire house. He decided to put tarpaper over our entire one and a half story house until he decided what would be best.

As he considered replacing the siding long term with another siding, the tarpaper took on a life of its own. Once the siding was protected, life got in the way. Dad seemed to forget to find new siding or to paint it.

Before I move on, let me say something about my Dad's talents. He was professionally skilled at building and remodeling, and was an excellent exterior and interior house painter. At work, he prided himself on custom color mixing to relieve the cookie cutter look of the homes he painted. That said, the interior of our house was constantly in some state of painting and remodeling. Many of the colors of our rooms were the colors of left over paint he brought home from work.

Back to my story...

Dad had good intentions to keep our house from structural failures, But the house looked like it was not finished—a house under construction year after year. This added to the impression in our community that we were a family in extreme poverty.

One Christmas our church brought us a holiday food basket. My mother refused it and told them to give it to someone who needed it. She said then, and many times after that, they probably thought it was false pride that she refused the basket.

At the time this food basket was delivered money was not a problem. Both of my parents were working at well-paying jobs. My parents were still growing some of our vegetables, or we picked vegetables at local truck farms. Any additional food stuffs we needed, especially for canning, Mom bought in large quantities from local farmers.

Added to this, Mom raised capon chickens for us and to sell. Lack of food was never a concern in our home.

Please, read more about the chickens in "Mom's Chicken, Cow and Ducks."

In all fairness to our town's people, given the community standards at the time, it is understandable that our town thought we were poor. Added to the appearance of our house, we had older cars and trucks. They were not clunkers, but very nice, just not new. Many people were in this same situation with cars, but added to our house, it continued the misconception of poverty.

Dad was a crack mechanic, his profession before he

went into interior house painting. He would buy older vehicles with good bodies and interiors at a fraction of their cost and then redo their mechanics and engines. If neighbors had new vehicles, they kept them for years, even without the extended warranties of today, since they had a good mechanic in the neighborhood.

Each of our vintage vehicles had some unique feature and we thoroughly enjoyed them. We had one convertible from the late forties that we enjoyed in the mid-fifties. It was like new inside and out. It had little seats with metal legs in both corners of the back. They could be folded up against the inside of the car giving more cargo room behind the front seats. They were perfect for my sister and me when all four of us were together.

Back to our house...

As you know, my mother had her cottage built in the late 1930s. For the first couple of years after their marriage my parents both worked and lived in the city during the week, and went to their cottage in the woods on weekends. They did not have me until nearly four years after their wedding. My sister was born the year after me.

With four of us, my parents wanted to live in the country but the two room cottage with an outhouse was not practical. They decided it needed to be expanded and include amenities like a fully operational kitchen and an inside bathroom.

When the new addition they designed was attached to the cottage, it had a huge kitchen, a sun porch with the original cottage rooms becoming the living room and the inside bathroom. The second floor was a half story that had two full bedrooms and two attics. They took advantage of the hilly lot by putting a walkout basement and a garage under the new addition and under the original cottage.

Even though my dad had the ability to build the addition himself, they hired it done. The addition included the shell of the house with roof, siding, windows, outside doors, and sub-flooring over the walk-out basement with a garage.

When the shell was completed, the roof sagged and the outside walls bowed out. There was no consumer protection then. They got nowhere with the builder to resolve the unsafe structure. Dad had to save the house from collapsing. They did not have any money to hire another contractor to fix it.

It was a set back for them, but once this was done, my parents worked on finishing the inside every spare moment they had. Doing this meant they met themselves coming and going some weeks with raising us and their full time work schedules.

Anyone who knew them as we did, knew their work on our house was a labor of love for our family.

Our upstairs was finished by the time I was seven. Until then, my sister and I slept in the main room of the original cottage. Eventually, it would become the living room when the new addition was completed and the upstairs could hold two double beds.

My parents slept upstairs from the moment the sub-flooring was completed, with bare walls with insulation and insulated wring facing them. Eventually, they had the two bedrooms walled in. This freed the living room area to be converted.

I remember my Dad carrying me upstairs to what would become my new bedroom. As he would tuck me in, he would call me his "sweetie pie" and kiss me on the forehead. After I was tucked in, we would say the *Lord's Prayer.*

As he went downstairs he was in silhouette by the glow of the lights that shown up from the kitchen. In the wintertime he would always look back over his shoulder and remind me to stay under the covers because it was cold.

It was, and I did.

When the upstairs bedrooms were finished, they were cozy. Each bedroom had two dormer windows that went out over the roof below. They opened in the middle like French doors.

Any work Dad did on the house left nothing to chance. The insulation he used exceeded the standards of that day and time because that was the top of the house and the furthest from the furnace in the basement.

The attics at each end of the upper story were floored and the walls were insulated. The center of the back attic had enough clearance for children that we could walk in it fully standing. There were many adventures in that attic when we were children. More on that later.

The new kitchen and the new walls ...

The new oversized kitchen meant the original cottage kitchen became our indoor bathroom. This relegated our outhouse to use for the men when there was a picnic or family reunion.

With World War II ending just after the cottage was built, building supplies for finishing the additional rooms were limited. But my parents prevailed.

The sheet rock in our new sun porch was supposedly of inferior quality. It was a takeoff of wood paneling. The sheet rock in the kitchen had a rough finish. We did not think of either of these as inferior grade. Instead, we thought it was quite nice. In modern times, many would like to have these "inferior" grade sheet rocks that was in our home.

Tile, tile, tile...

I recall the Saturday we laid the tile in our kitchen. The kitchen was the central room that all traffic went through to get to any part of the house. This meant some logistical planning to get the room done without totally interrupting household activities such as using the bathroom. Preparing food ahead of time kept us fed. The challenges my parents handled with their usual organizational and capable abilities.

Fortunately, during some of the delays, we had the outhouse and our old pump for water. Although I did not think so at the time, all things considered it was an exhilarating experience.

Once the kitchen was floored, a few months later Dad constructed a set of built-in shelves and drawers at the end of the kitchen. Then he painted the kitchen walls and the cupboards and drawers to match. It was his practice as an excellent house painter to use the same color for the woodwork using a semi-gloss paint. His philosophy was that this same color paint would make any room look larger.

The living room...

The living room which had been our bedroom for years, kept the same walls and rough-hewn flooring for many years after it became our living room.

In 1956, my Gramma Louisa and I watched soap operas in this living room. She was elderly by this time and I was one of her youngest grandchildren. It was a special time for me.

In the history of television, there were not many soap operas to watch but enough to make some choices. Her favorites were *As the World Turns* and *Guiding Light*. To this day, while other soaps are interesting to me, these two remain my favorites.

When Gramma was near the end of her life, her children decided my mother was best equipped to care for her. We moved a hospital bed in the living room for her. I would turn on her favorite soap operas in the afternoon and sit with her. She was oblivious to the soaps at this point, but who is to know what bits and pieces of something she liked gave her joy.

After Gramma's passing, Dad decided to remodel the living room and bring it into more modern decor, he put in a big picture window with little window panes. Then he chose knotty pine for the walls. Most knotty pine walls of that time were finished in a dark stain. He decided to use a light honey-colored stain that he had seen used on the outside of houses in the city. This way the knots in the pine showed up in contrast to the light finish.

Before the walls were done, the ceiling had been done years before. It was composed of smooth cream interlocking white acoustical ceiling blocks. Difficult to get at the time they did it. They had cost a premium, but to my parents it was worth it, since they were both originally from the city. This ceiling when finished would have been welcome in any elegant city house. Please, read more about this ceiling a bit later in this story.

Added to these walls and ceiling was an unusual deep blue rug that my parents found in the corner of a carpet store. It was a wool carpet that had the same design on both sides. When one side was worn, the other side could be used. It fit the room dimensions exactly giving the appearance of wall-to-wall carpeting.

The room was a masterpiece. We sat on the new carpeted floor for a day just admiring the walls and carpet before we put the furniture back in it.

Attic adventures and the living room ceiling...

The attics at each end of the upper story had treasures for us. Our parents did not mind our being in the attic. We would get whatever it was we wanted and go play in our room or somewhere else in the house.

When I was nine or ten, always the willful child, our big attic had a lure for me that would change our living room. We had been told not to walk off the floored part of either of the attics. But I saw some boxes at the back of the attic that I wanted to get into. My sister told me not to go to the back of the attic. Being the oldest, she could not dissuade me. I assured her that I would walk on the beams. Not to worry.

Balancing on the beams, I tried to reach for a box. My arm could not quite reach it and I lost my balance. I slipped through the living room ceiling blocks. For some reason that remains a mystery to this day, I did not fall through to the floor below.

Apparently, I held on to the beams as my sister ran to the basement to get our mother. Mom, in the midst of doing laundry, left the wringer washer unattended. As she ran upstairs, she could hear me screaming. As she ran into the living room, all she could see were my legs kicking.

She stood under me in the living room and yelled up at me so that I would stop kicking and screaming. The more I moved, the chances were I would fall through the hole in the ceiling. For some reason she could not pull me through to catch me.

Once I was calm, she rushed upstairs and pulled me up through the hole. She saved me. Then she spanked me.

My parents were glad that I did not get hurt. But both my parents were discouraged that their ceiling was damaged. Dad fixed the hole with four new slightly rougher finished ceiling tiles. He tried to find the exact replacement tiles but was unsuccessful but they matched in color. Over the years we did not notice the difference in the tiles unless we were recalling the story of how I fell through the ceiling.

Our house gets a painted face...

A few years after the food basket incident, Dad was laid-off from his house painting job. When it seemed apparent, he would not get a job in the city any time soon, he took small remodeling and painting jobs in our town and the surrounding area.

That spring, my second cousins who owned the cottage down the road from our house, hired Dad to paint their cottage. It was long overdue for a paint job.

And being among year-round, well-kept houses, it was starting to look run down.

Please, read more about the cousins and their cottage in "Summer Cottages."

This was probably a job that was in part to help our family. Our relatives were that way. They knew that my mother had become the mainstay of our family's income. If it was a "put-up" job, Dad did not seem to notice or care. He was enthused to go to a job he could walk to and from after all his equipment was in place.

The exterior of the cottage was novelty siding. The same siding that was under our tarpaper. The restoration took a few months and three coats of paint. Some of the siding and trim boards had to be ordered and replaced.

Our cousins did not seem to mind. They knew Dad's work was above and beyond the average. And, it looked like new when it was finished. As it turned out, this paint job lasted years past what had been expected.

As this cottage took on such a new look, my parents decided to take the tarpaper off the back of our house to check the condition of the siding. It looked nearly new. They thought they might paint the back of the house and see what the outcome would be. When it was like new, they decided to paint the entire house white, which was its original color. It took two coats of paint but did not need anything replaced since it had been protected for so many years.

After the house was painted, Dad thought it needed shutters. He used the leftover knotty pine boards from the living room walls. He bought turquoise paint on sale for the shutters and the house's trim paint.

When Dad finished with the outside of our house, it was beautiful. We had always known what a special house our parents had created. Now the rest of the community knew.

In the years before this, as we would get off the school bus, every now and then, someone would ask us when our house was going to be finished. We were embarrassed. My sister would not comment to such crass remarks.

But when I heard such comments, I would tell school

chum making such an insensitive comment that it was finished. Because it had a roof, walls, windows and doors. And everything in it worked. The tarpaper was just there to protect the siding until our father decided what he wanted to do with the outside.

It fell on deaf ears.

When we went to school the fall after our house was painted, as we boarded the bus, the bus driver commented on how nice our house looked. And the school kids on the bus looked out the windows wide-eyed in amazement. Several openly oooohed and ahhhhed about the new look of our house. One of the older kids said it looked like we had come into money. We just smiled.

Our tarpaper house was not gone. It became a polished gem.

Country Living—Marshmallows, Pets, a Stone Fireplace, the Sulfur Pump and Water Pails, and My Sister in the Corner

After reading "My Hometown" and "Our Tarpaper House" you already know some of the wonderful things that happened in our day-to-day lives.

In the 1940s, 50s and 60s, we lived in the country at a time when the suburbs were beginning to be where city folks wanted to live. Living further out in the country was not yet vogue. But it was us.

Locust trees were plentiful in our yard. Their fragrance was lovely when they were in full bloom and was similar to honeysuckle.

My parents named our property Locust Acres. Dad made a sign that was hung at the beginning of our driveway. It was turquoise with gold letters spelling Locust Acres. For many years, we even put that name on address labels.

Before the naming and the sign, in the early days of living in the country we had an unusual mailbox at the corner of our gravel driveway. It was a wooden structure that was triangle-shaped. The top bar was big enough that from time to time my dad sat my sister and me on it while he got the mail. On one occasion we posed for Mom to take a picture of the three of us and our childhood dog, Tippy. A picture that has always been special to our family.

Pets, pets, pets...

No memory of our country living would be complete without remembering our family pets. We had our share of cats, dogs, an occasional parakeet, and an assortment of gold fish. All our dogs and cats were affectionate. None were pedigreed but a few came close. Regardless of their heritage, we took good care of all of them, but some were more special to us than others.

Tippy was one of the special ones. He was a taffy-colored Spits and Fox Terrier combination with some other small breeds mixed in. He was our dog from our toddler years until we were teenagers.

Sadly, one day he raced out to be with my dad to get the mail and was hit by a car. We decided Tippy should be buried under a shade tree near the small creek that ran between our property and our unusual woods. Tippy's final resting place began that spot as our family's pet cemetery. After that, any cat or dog we had that passed while living with us joined him.

Among our many cats, we had one that was a mostly a long-haired Persian. She had kittens and we found homes for all of them. One of her babies was totally black. When I told my seventh grade teacher about this cat and its almost Persian heritage, she said she wanted it. My mother and she talked and it seemed a sincere request and commitment.

Bockmier was named after her last name. We did not want to give him a personal pet name and get attached to him. When he was about three months old and weaned, we called my former teacher. Her kitten was ready to go to his new home. She said she was sorry but things in her life had changed and she could not take him.

By this time, regardless of our intentions, we were attached to him. Our family decided to keep him. Bockmier kept his name and stayed with us for many years until he caught cat leukemia. We had to put him to sleep. Something we were undone doing. He went to our family pet cemetery with Tippy.

But overall, when we could not keep a cat or dog, my mother would try to find someone who wanted them or she called the SPCA. When she called them, she would tell us she found a farmer who took our pets. We accepted that.

At times, we would ask to go visit the pet. Mom would discourage us saying something about it being unfair to the dog or cat and their adjustment to their new family. When we were adults, we finally let her know we figured out what she had done. She never confessed. When questioned about the truth, she just smiled her smile.

Water, water, water...

The stream next to our pet cemetery emptied into a creek just around the corner on the next road. That creek was almost deep enough to swim in. A few times each summer we neighborhood kids and any visiting cousins would go down to the deep creek and wade and sort of swim around with the water up to our shoulders. Or, we would catch tadpoles.

The pump...

As I have written earlier, during the early years of my parent's marriage they grew vegetables and fruits, carrying water to the fields if rain was not plentiful. This water came from our sulfur pump. And, the sulfur water was piped into the house for laundry and use in our bathroom. It had a strong odor but it was pure water, and we were grateful to have it.

However, drinking it was not something we wanted to do. Even boiling would not take that smell or taste away. For drinking water our neighbors willingly shared their cool well water with us.

My father always mumbled and grumbled that our water was pure until the neighbors across the street, who were downhill, dug their well. But that was never proven. Today our old pump is covered with a wisteria vine and rhododendron bushes my mother planted around and over it once it was no longer used.

Back when we hauled water, my mother was proud of the gleaming porcelain pails she had for drinking water. She handled them with kid gloves to and from gathering the drinking and cooking water from across the street several times a week.

After we were five, Mom or Dad would let us help pump the water. But they always carried it home. One night around dusk, when I was six or seven, I begged Mom to let me carry one of the pails home. I was big for my age, and really thought I could carry one pail all the way.

She was hesitant. But it was the end of the day, and she was carrying two pails. One was smaller and new. We walked up the neighbor's drive way to the road. All the while I continued to beg to carry the pail full of water. Just as we began down the road to our house I asked one last time.

Finally, she gave in. She gently set both pails on the edge of the road's pavement. She stopped before she handed me the smaller pail and sternly said, "If it gets too heavy, stop and tell me. Don't drop this pail on the road, it's new and I don't want it chipped."

I nodded my head in a promise.

About the time we approached our driveway, my dad came to the door of our walk-out basement. The child in me dropped the pail on the road and ran to be hugged by him. When I was half way to him, my mother's hand swooped upon me from behind and she began spanking me for dropping *and* chipping her new pail.

It was a few days before she stopped scowling at me. But life goes on.

Picnics, our stone fireplace, soda pop and marshmallows...

We ate outside for dinner almost every day in the summer. It did not have to be a special occasion. Nor did we have to have family visiting, although we had that, Gramma Louisa, aunts, uncles, cousins, and friends who were like family at any given time. Living in the country then was similar in the large number of visitors as it is to those people who now live in resort areas. The company seems to be never ending. But we liked it.

One of our family's friends owned a neighborhood grocery store in the city. Their family would make a day of it in the country with us. They brought us New York hot dogs and buns, delicatessen salads and treated us to all flavors of soda pop. We put the pop in a galvanized tub with ice.

And, on any given day, we sat or lay quietly on the lawn and watched the clouds roll by. We would not even have to talk to each other. It was that kind of time.

At the center of this picnic activity was our stone fireplace. It was up on our hill near our picnic table. My dad planned and built every inch of it. It was a work of art that was the centerpiece for many a gathering, barbecue, picnic or family reunion.

Many of our relatives and friends with much more affluent houses were a bit envious of this fine work and the food it produced. If nothing was cooking on it, my dad would gladly build a small fire and we would roast marshmallows.

Marshmallows...

He had a special way for us to roast marshmallows.

Green branches were the only way to roast marshmallows according to Dad. He instructed us on the gathering and leaf removal. An art in itself, and it was. Most times, we put our marshmallows on a green branch because they bowed toward the fire and we could hang it very close to the embers without touching the flames of the fire.

"Most people put the marshmallow too close to the fire," he would say.

The secret, according to him, was to get the marshmallow to turn a medium dark brown. Which meant the inside was melted and the warm insides were contained by this bronzed outer surface.

"No need to get it burnt and black to get it roasted and soft," he told us every time.

Marshmallows melting in our mouths would satisfy our sweet tooth for days.

My quiet sister in the corner...

My sister, being the good one, did not do things we call childhood hijinx. You have already read about some of these in "Our Tarpaper House." Please, read more about these adventures and hijinx in "The Toaster" and "Summer Cottages." And to me she was one of those children who thought if she closed her eyes you could not see her.

We usually played together, the boy down the road, the girl across the road, my sister and me. In the years just before we started school, on some of our play days my mother would string up clothes under the regular clotheslines halfway down the Locust trees. We would hang our washed doll clothes on them.

On other days, we girls, that could include the girl across the road and my visiting girl cousin who outgrew her *bad seed* years, would dig in a cedar trunk of old evening gowns from the 1940s. Whatever combination of girls were there, we dressed up for the day. Some days we just played with dolls, had the usual tea parties and stayed close to my mother, grandmother, my father or all three.

At times being the older three children—the boy down the road, the girl across the road and me—we would leave my sister out of our play. as I reacll one summer day they were both at our house. The day my sister disappeared.

It was a summer Saturday like most others. My father was working overtime in the city. Gramma was there, which meant breakfast included Mom's special Belgian waffles with pecans. Then everyone went about their day.

Suddenly, my mother and grandmother were scurrying around calling for my sister. The three of us heard them outside and came to the side screen door.

Mom and Gramma simultaneously shouted, "Your sister is missing!"

Not many had phones, so calling for others to help us look for her was not an option. There was no time to personally contact neighbors. That time was best used looking for my sister.

Gramma and Mom had checked the upstairs bedrooms and were going to the basement. We three agreed to go to the woods next to the house and look for her. We ran to the woods calling her name.

By this time, my mother and grandmother were outside calling her name as they went through the other two woods to the side and back of our house. Finally, we all met back at the house. We were exhausted.

Both women decided to go inside and get some ice water for all of us. Just then I heard Gramma say, "Vera, look over there."

Mom looked in the phone corner of the dining area of our kitchen. There sat my sister in a chair.

We three came into the house to get some water. When we did, we saw my sister sitting still like a mannequin. My mother asked her if she heard all of us calling for her. She had, but thought if she sat there and waited, we would find her.

The ironic part of all this, when my mother had checked the upstairs bedrooms she passed this spot. To this day, no one really knows if my sister was there the entire time, not even my sister.

She was not sure if she had fallen asleep in some obscure spot like under a bed and woke when we were calling her name. Or, if she was playing a game by hiding from us. Then decided to go to the corner of the dining room from wherever she was while we were all frantically searching for her outside.

For years when anyone in our family, or a close family friend used the expression "quiet as a mouse," Mom added as she looked at my sister, "Or, someone in the corner."

The Toaster – Tonsils, the Kitchen Cabinet, Bee Stings and Childhood Accidents

Like many children we had our share of childhood accidents. You have already read about some of them in "Our Tarpaper House."

The toaster...

One of my mother's best friends throughout her life lived a short distance down the road. She was the mother of the boy down the road. Back then they shared babysitting between them. Other times we just played at each other's homes. The house rules at both our homes was that neither mother allowed running or horseplay in the house. But things happen, kids will be kids.

Our neighbor had an immaculate, organized house at all times. Her kitchen and dining area off the kitchen had some custom features. There was a pass through under her cupboard to put food into the dining area. A cupboard above the pass through opened both into the kitchen and the dining room. The dining area held a large oak table that would seat her family of five comfortably, and a few extra packed.

Their toaster was always in the dining room to make it handy for breakfast. Most days the toaster was put away for the rest of the day, because to use it there the cord was across the walking area around the table. One of the days we were playing in the dining room, it was left in the dining room with the cord still plugged in.

It was a Saturday and a play day. Just before we were to go outside one thing led to another. We began running in the house. Not thinking because I was being chased, I ran around the table and knocked their new toaster onto floor.

We told his mother immediately, and she tried to be calm. New things for her family were not as difficult as they were for our family. But they were not easy.

We all waited until her husband came in from his yard chores to see if the toaster was all right. Upon careful inspection the bottom door that opens to clean out the crumbs was slightly dented. But the toaster seemed unharmed. Time would tell.

We never heard that the toaster was broken, and presumed it worked for years after that. But I was "in the dog house," not those chasing me, just me, for a while whenever I was there even playing outside. It made me feel bad that this happened, so I tried to be on my best behavior.

Please, read more about Mom's friend in "Mom's Barely Soup."

The kitchen cabinet...

Years before the toaster incident when I was sixish, Gramma Louisa was staying with us for one of her biannual visits.

I was trying to get something on a top shelf of our

kitchen cabinet. A time or two, I had stood on the bottom shelf, trying to reach something higher up and my mother pulled me off the cabinet. She scolded me for doing that as my Gramma looked on. They cautioned me that the cabinet was not secured to the wall and could fall on me.

Gramma stood there crossing her arms in front of her chest, silently nodding her head in affirmation. My mother told me not only could I get hurt, even worse, I could die from the cabinet and its contents falling on me.

We all three agreed this was something I should not do. But instead, I should either ask Gramma or Mom to get what I wanted. My agreement was remembered by me for a day or two, maybe even a week. The day came when I saw something on the top shelf and did not want to wait for one of them to help me. I stepped up on the bottom shelf to reach for it.

This time was different. I did not expect anything unusual to happen. After all, I had climbed up on this cabinet many times without any disaster. But this time, the cabinet began to fall away from the wall. As it toppled over. I can still recall the canned goods and boxes falling out on me and falling passed me on each side to the floor.

Within seconds I was laying on the kitchen floor pinned under this mess. I was screaming for help. I tried to push it all off me and crawl out. Not possible.

Within seconds, but what seemed like a long time, my mother was there, pushing the cabinet up off me. Gramma was pulling me out from under the cabinet and lifting me up off the floor onto my feet. As she did this, the canned goods and boxes fell from me to the floor, joining the stuff already there.

They checked me to make sure I was not hurt. Once they could see that I was all right, the scolding began.

I never did that again. And I was lucky no harm came to me. Later I heard that people died from doing this. That must have scared me straight.

Please, read more about Gramma's visits in "My Two Grammas."

The snap...

Around this same time in my life as the kitchen cabinet caper, I was playing with my mother's button and snap collection while she was sewing. I saw a shiny snap and decided to put it in my ear like my Gramma's hearing aid. It set there for a few minutes. But when I tried to get it out, it went back into my ear.

I went into the living room where I tried to dig at it with a crochet hook. It went further in. I did not want to tell my mother what I had done. I said nothing to my parents.

As a child, I figured it would work its way out sooner or later—just drop out of my ear. Did not happen. Instead, I developed a severe ear infection.

Nothing my mother did to treat it made it go away. Finally, my parents decided to take me to Dr. Cooper. My father took me to the doctor's office.

He looked in my ear and told my father he saw a piece of metal in my ear. Then he asked me, "Young lady, did you put something in your ear?"

I kept silent.

He worked carefully to extract the metal object, since it rested on my ear drum. When he got it out, he and my father were amazed. Then I confessed as to what I had done.

He put medicine in my ear. Shook his head and said, "We'll have to see if there is any scar tissue and long term damage to her hearing."

Then he leaned down close to my face and said, "From now on, young lady, nothing goes into your ear smaller than your elbow."

I nodded a "yes."

When I got home, my mother ranted and I cried. "Why did you do it? Why didn't you tell us?"

And, so on. Somewhere between their questions and my crying, I told them I wanted to have a hearing aid like my Gramma. Kids.

The years go on. My parents would put the medicine in my ear and it would clear up. But not for long, I had ear infections that would come and go more often than most people have colds and hay fever.

The Indian Reservation and a new doctor...

Shortly after the ear incident, my mother began working as a nurse at the Seneca Indian Reservation. During this time the ear infections were at their worst. The doctor at the Indian Reservation treated me with penicillin shots every week sometimes for a month at a time.

The first time he saw me for this infection, he laid the needle out where it could be seen. Our family doctor was more concealing when he gave shots. The first shot this new doctor gave me was so forceful, it left a square black and blue mark on my behind. After that, we chuckled as we alternated sides for shots based on the black and blue mark as our guide.

When the ears were infected, we had to gently push gauze inside as far as we could to absorb it. This also gave me relief from pain. And, I slept for years with a hot water bottle to control the pain of these ear aches.

Because of this condition, it was necessary as I grew up to not to get in a draft, even in the summer playing outside. If this was not done, I would have an earache, and without fail, an ear infection. I finally outgrew the ear problems when I was in junior high.

The pool...

Being family of a medical staffer did not count when we asked to go in the pool. Mom, was empathetic, she would not even ask if we could swim in the pool. It was built for the Indians by our government. And, that was that. Mom had a good set of ethics and was a stickler for no exceptions to the rules.

Tonsils, tonsils, tonsils...

Next and all through the ear problems we had our tonsillectomies. We were six and seven and we were told the usual. "When you get your tonsils out, you can have all the ice cream you can eat."

Dr. Cooper has said we should get them out years before we did. As it turned out, my mother had a small amount of medical benefits as a coworker at the Indian Reservation. As I got older, there may have been mention that the surgeon's fee was very modest to her family and the hospital bill was discounted.

When her doctor boss and she decided to do the operation, they decided to schedule my sister and me on the same day. This meant my mother could take a week off work and nurse us at the same time.

We went to the Gowanda Hospital for the surgery. This hospital was quite a distance in those days from our home, but closer than those in Buffalo. We went in the night before and were to come home by the day after the surgery. Two nights in the hospital was intimidating but Mom was with us.

My sister was put in a crib. But I was big for my age and they put in a room across the hall in a bed. The hospital did not think a crib would hold me.

We chuckled about that for years. Why? When my mother stayed the night with us, she got tired of sleeping in a chair. She crawled into the empty crib in my sister's room and slept the night. At that time my mother weighed close to two hundred pounds.

Surgery time came and the prep for it began.

As the story goes, my sister was so resistant to the pre-anesthesia they had to give her a medication rectally that subdued her without harm. Then to get her to sleep, she had to count backwards from one hundred. She got to ten before she fell off to sleep.

I went to sleep in seconds. I can still do that, any where, any time.

My sister's surgery went quickly, but mine was another story. When the time began to get long, my mother knowingly became concerned. She began to fret and pace.

Finally, the doctor came out after the surgery and explained. He said it took almost triple the time and told my mother that my scar tissue from so many infections had to be removed before the tonsils. It took two surgeons nearly a half hour to remove it and then another half hour for him to remove the tonsils and adenoids.

She was relieved. Her chickies would be all right.

After the surgery, to make it easy on my mother, they rolled my sister's crib in with me for the night and told my mother to use the other bed. The three of us were together and we slept well considering the pain my sister and I had.

All the ice cream you can eat...

If memory serves, we did not want to eat anything, not even ice cream. Instead, we lay in our beds moaning and groaning. By dinner time they brought us the smallest bowl of vanilla ice cream I have ever seen before or since. That was it.

When my father came to visit us after work, we were still drowsy. My mother walked him to the door and kissed him goodbye.

A few minutes after they left my room, I decided to follow them. The nurses found me looking for my parents in a waiting room of strangers with my gown flapping open in the back. I was walked back to my room, where my mother was frantic looking for her missing child.

The boy and girl across the street and their tonsils...

The year before our tonsillectomies, when they had their tonsils out, it was at the same time, too. Their affluent grandparents and parents filled their joint recovery bedroom with toys that rivaled Christmas. This memory gave us false expectations when we agreed to have our tonsils out.

Although "all the ice cream you could eat" was promised, what excited us prior to the surgery were visions of our bedroom being filled with toys. Like the neighbor kids, a second Christmas.

But our grandparents were not in a position to lavish even small amounts of toys on us. Maybe we had some new coloring books, crayons and small things from the 5 & 10 cent store. That was about it.

Ice cream was a food luxury our parents could not afford. But we did have all the homemade pudding and Jello we could eat. Mom had a recipe that made her homemade cooked smooth and creamy chocolate pudding. She put it in her and our favorite elegant stemmed pudding dishes.

Then I took a month longer to heal than the average tonsillectomy. The doctor thought it had to do with all the scar tissue I had. He and my parents knew this might be somewhat more painful, with slight nerve damage and all.

Every time I drank or tried to eat soup, I had an odd sensation. It felt like it was going up my Eustachian tubes and come out my nose or ears. It was a weird and painful sensation, probably due to the complications of my ear infections. No one ever really knew, nor did I.

The neighborhood kids chided me when I claimed this continuing discomfort. They were not sympathetic, after all they had recovered in weeks, as had my sister. None of the neighborhood children or my sister really knew I had the scar tissue complication.

The boy down the road...

No story about our neighborhood would be complete without telling about the day the boy down the road was injured.

He decided to run alongside his uncle mowing the

fields back behind our houses. No one but the boy knows why he was running alongside the tractor. As the tractor turned, the uncle did not see or hear him. He was caught in those strong cornflower blue flowers with a rope like stems. He could not run out of the way. The grass cutting blade almost cut through his left arm.

He was six. They rushed him home, packed his arm in ice. And, then rushed him to the nearest hospital in Lackawana, New York some twenty miles away.

We prayed.

In those days, the only real alternative to save his life at that emergency room was to stop the bleeding and amputate. The first few years after this accident, there was some talk about the hospital not being the best in the area. The neighborhood consensus was that a more advanced hospital of the time and their surgeons might (key word might) have been able to try to reattach the arm so that he would have full use.

Back then one hospital did not try to stabilize a patient and transport them to the one in the area that had the more advanced technology. This was before high speed cars and ambulances, interstate highways and hospital air lift helicopters.

This boy was (and still is) such a gentle soul, loved by the neighborhood. We seldom even thought about his arm being half gone. We had him. That was all that mattered.

He and his parents qualified for an artificial arm through a children's foundation at the time. He and his mother flew to Michigan to get the arm fitted. And, he was taught how to use it.

As his body grew, they refitted him with a new arm. By his adult years he was in his third arm. Our high school physical education teacher marveled at how he expected no special consideration. He just asked for extra time to shower.

His parents were the key to this. They made every effort not to make him to think of himself as disabled. They expected him to do as his brother and sister did around the house and at school.

And, he lived up to that expectation.

The only time we saw any pampering, was on hot summer days. It was years before home air conditioning was routine. They would let him take off his arm to be cool. He would relax in the house or play in his yard without it.

As an adult, he is a very successful father, husband and computer programmer. I barely can use a computer with two hands. I commented to him once, that it amazed me that he was so skilled in computers with one hand. Even more awesome, he fully participated in raising his children. He takes life joyously in stride and savors every moment.

Two wheelers...

After and through all the illnesses, operations and lifesaving and tricycles we had our first two wheelers. Read more about the boy down the road's trike in "Childhood Antics."

Our first two wheel bikes were miniature red and white bikes.

My mother was so proud of us, and pleased with how we looked that she dressed us in our new Easter dresses she had made and posed us with our bikes. She took "formal" pictures of each of us. From them, she made a composite photo and sent them with our Christmas cards.

We rode these two-wheelers with training wheels for the longest time. As our riding improved, my dad moved the training wheels up higher to use more as kickstands. After that, he left one training wheel on the left side, as a kick stand.

One summer day, the grampa, who lived with the boy down the road challenged me, "You can't ride that bike without those training wheels."

He always goaded me. This is the same the grampa who tricked me into snorting snuff when I was sevenish. I was so sick. The neighbors who went to my church promised to hold a glass of milk in the back of the Bible School audience when I did my Bible verses, just in case.

When he said this to me, I insisted I could ride the bike without training wheels. The one was just left on to be used as a kick stand. He continued to insist I could not ride without it.

Furious, I rode home and had my dad take the training wheel off my bike, against his better judgment. Before this, I rode the bike without wavering. At first, when I started down the road, I was swerving from side to side. By the time I got to Grampa Tony, I was riding with a steady control. He had his way about him, as he chuckled when I showed him the last remaining training wheel was off.

The bike pack...

My next bike was a twenty-inch Roadmaster, a sturdy bike that was quite the bike of that time. Having a bike like that, got me in with the older kids in the neighborhood. They had a bike riding pack.

The pack of bikers who rode up and down our country road were like a school of fish on many spring, summer and fall days. Even though we were not close to all the cyclists, when a group of friends were riding, we were joined by other children at will. Some of the cyclists were visiting relatives from the city for the day or weekend, or were staying in the country for the summer. Four would become six and six would become eight, and so on.

Our rural road was prone to speeders even in the cars of yesteryear. But we could be seen from one small hill near the boy down the road's house all the way to the steep hill toward the other end of the road. The road that intersected ours was a stop road, with a blind corner. Cars stopped there rather than get hit. We were not in jeopardy from that road as we biked along.

As long as we stayed in the open on the flat stretch of our road, we could ride back and forth up and down the road harm free for hours. And, the cars that did come along were respectful of us and us of them.

Unfortunately, one afternoon we decided to go further than the flat stretch we usually rode. We biked up the steep hill. And, we biked down.

Coming down was faster than anticipated. My bike was near the right side of the road. But, I was worried that a bike or two on the left of me would come down too fast and hit me. I looked over my left shoulder to see what I could see.

Just then, my bicycle hit a bump and I was thrown over the handlebars onto the pavement. I landed on my face. The bikers stopped, throwing their bikes to the ground and ran to me. The oldest ones helped me up and walked me to the nearest house which was at the base of this hill. The younger riders waited at

the entrance to that driveway.

The young eighteen something woman who lived there with her parents opened the door. She was visibly upset to see me, a child with a bleeding face being held up by two pre-teens. She called to her mother for help. Her mother brought me inside and packed my face with a towel full of ice to stop the bleeding. Then she told her daughter to walk me home, slowly and to keep my head as level as she could while keeping the ice on my face. And, she said, keep awake and talk to her.

They had no car at home to drive me and no phone. The older children ran ahead to tell my mother what had happened.

Alert, I could feel two of my teeth on the back left side were broken. Split and hanging like a hinged flap. I could put my tongue between them and swing them open from each other.

Two days after the accident, my parents took me to our family dentist. He took both teeth out. He told my parents luckily these were my first teeth and that my second teeth would come in on time. The second teeth were not damaged.

Oddly, I had little or no pain in those broken teeth. Or, perhaps I was in such face pain, I did not notice.

Back to my story ...

I tried to tell the gal walking me home that my teeth were broken. But she insisted I not talk. She kept the ice on my chin and held my head as level as he could, just as her mother had told her to do. Even then people knew this was a head injury.

My mother ran to meet us. She kept the ice on my face and took me into the house. She called Dr. Cooper's office in Angola, and told him what had happened. He would be expecting us.

My dad had our only car. She continued holding the ice on my face and called a neighbor to take us to the doctor. The ice was on my face until the doctor saw me.

We did not have to wait as we usually did. We rushed past the waiting room full of patients who had sat there for hours to be first come first served. This was an emergency.

The doctor and my mother cleaned my face. He stitched my face as she assisted. Then he stitched my chin skin closed and emptied his bandage supply on my face. In his cautious state he wanted to keep my face in place, lest there be any ripped or torn muscles that must heal with support.

I felt like a mummy. The hard bandages were like a beard and mustache. It was so firm like a cast, that I could not talk or open my mouth but a crack.

My sister had waited in the waiting room with our neighbor. My dad came as soon as he came home from work and read the note that we were at the doctor's office.

Once assured I was all right, he wanted to take me for a soft drink. The nearest place to go was the bowling alley. We did not go in there as a rule, because a tavern was attached. But we did that night.

The soft drink was too cold for me. My dad had them take out the ice. Only then I was able to sip it slowly, very slowly. When I got home, I could only eat lukewarm soups for a week, and pudding and Jello.

Our doctor had advised my mother to immediately get a plastic surgeon on this. I remember him saying, "If this was a boy, we could let it heal on its own. But a girl should have plastic surgery."

Plastic surgery and me...

My parents had no medical coverage. Plastic surgery. They felt it was necessary. But how?

My mother called in all her doctor and nurse markers. She could not get free plastic surgery. But she located one of the best plastic surgeons for that time in Buffalo. And, my parents were able to pay him $10 a month for what seemed like forever.

In the beginning, the plastic surgeon examined me and the terms were agreed on. We went the next week for the surgery.

They gave me a local anesthetic, but did not test me to see if I was numb. The pins and needles sensation that I felt in comparison was second only to labor pains.

The plastic surgeon determined that I did not have any muscle tears. He concentrated on the chin. I left with a much smaller bandage. More like a goatee. Still stiff like a cast.

It was a long drive to Buffalo in those days of slower cars. A time or two during follow up visits we took the bus to and from the city. On those hot summer days, the bus seemed even slower, more tedious and uncomfortable than usual with a bandaged face.

Over the next few months when we went to the city for my check-ups, the bandages got smaller and smaller. Finally, the stitches were to come out. Most of them came out smoothly. But one was elusive. The doctor pulled at it several times and my face went with each pull.

Then he said, "Oh, well, that one will have to work it way out on its own."

From then on, and for the year that followed, we put coca butter on my chin nightly to help diminish the scar.

As I got older, I was convinced that the thumb print size cleft in my chin was due to the accident. But my dad told me that people's faces return to their original state in less than five years after plastic surgery. And, my baby and toddler pictures did have a small cleft showing that I had not noticed before. It was not the plastic surgery after all.

The school bus and the stairs...

Some years after the bike accident on a winter's day came my adventures at a neighborhood girlfriend's house. They had added an upstairs bedroom to their house. A bigger bedroom for their only child.

She was older than I was, but a closer friend to my sister than to me. When we rode the school bus together, she would sit with my sister. They found all kinds of things to talk about.

Please, read more about this neighborhood girl in Halloween of Days Gone By and my sister's costumes.

She was a good girl, not a devilish bone in her body. But the boys on the bus were another story. One afternoon they lit her ponytail on fire. I saw it and warned her and we put it out.

They had gone too far. The bus driver drove us all the way back to school even though we were about halfway through our route. We unloaded and sat in a classroom until the boys either confessed or we told who they were. I am not sure which happened. But the two boys were expelled for a week.

Back to my story...

A few years before the bus incident, a group of neighborhood girls played together at one of the older girl's house. Some of the time her girl cousins would visit from the city. We were all upstairs in the girl's new bedroom. The door to the bedroom was not on yet. The parents warned us to be careful not to slip or fall down the stairs.

In the course of events, we decided to play Blind Man's Bluff. I was chosen to be "it." Before I was blindfolded, I was promised by the older girls there that someone would stand by the opening to the stairs. As I neared the stairs, they forgot their promise and scattered.

When they saw me approach the stairs, they screamed for me to stop. In my blindfolded state, all I heard was screaming and continued toward the open door area and the stairs

Their yelling "stop" just blended with their screams as I tried to find them in the room. Since I would not stop, someone reached up and took the blindfold off, thinking I would open my eyes. When I did not open my eyes, they began yelling to me to open my eyes. But I had the sensation the blindfold was still on me.

Suddenly, I rolled down the stairs. I opened my eyes when I landed.

The girl's mother, who had heard the screaming, was at my side when I landed. She made me sit there and told me not move. That was easy to do because I felt like I had broken something. She called my mother. Mom had a car by this time and raced to this house.

She checked me over and I was walking and talking. They decided I must not have broken anything. I was in pain but that was understandable, they said.

They helped me put on my coat, gloves, hat and scarf. The pain was so bad in my hands, it hurt to put on my mittens. Once again, we drove to our family doctor's office. Again, I was rushed past the waiting room full of people.

Back then no X-rays were taken. If you were moving, they presumed that nothing was broken, cracked, ripped or torn. Within a day, I was black and blue and swollen all over my body for weeks. The doctor ordered bed rest and aspirin for pain. For months it continued to hurt my skin as I pulled my clothes on, especially my heavy woolen winter clothes to go outside.

The pain, the agony.

As a child I was not very popular with the neighborhood children, a bit of a scapegoat at times. Over the years I always felt the girls did not try all that hard to stop my fall.

All these many years later, I still feel that way. To my recollection, as most children do, they doctored their version of what happened to keep from getting punished by their parents. They went too far. After all two of the girls were older and taller than I was. Yet, no one reached out and grabbed me to keep me from falling.

Bees stings...

On other days, especially summer days, we had some mysteries to solve. Or so we thought.

It was late August, and the boy down the road said his brother was going to drown their kittens in the pond near the big woods. We were not sure if this was a reality or a spoof his older brother was playing on him.

This was the same brother who had convinced his younger brother that a bar of soap was a bar of candy to such an extent the boy down the road started to eat it. His parents discovered this activity in time to stop him from any serious harm but he was very sick for a couple days.

We, including the girl across the road, my sister and I decided to play in the fields back by the big woods so that we could watch for the brother. We did not see him go buy us, but off in the distance we heard the older brother's old jitney. It sounded like it was in the woods headed in the direction of the pond.

The four of us, fearful that he would make good on his promise to drown the kittens, ran up into the big woods toward the pond. But the sound we thought to be his older brother got ahead of us. We wandered around in the woods trying to pick up the noise of the jitney. All of a sudden bees were buzzing around all of us. We were swatting bees from around our heads. We had unknowingly stomped on an underground German bees' nest.

When we realized that we were surrounded by bees and being stung, we all took off running like crazed animals. We ran uncontrollably without stopping, even though we thought we would drop. But the adrenaline was pumping and we made it out of the woods and we noticed the bees stopped chasing us halfway down the fields.

We ran toward my house for help. It was acres from where we were, but the closet house among us. Once we arrived at the house, my mother was not home and it was locked. In our panic, we forgot we had been playing at the neighbor boy's house while my mother was doing errands.

The next nearest house for help was the neighbor girl's across the road. We rushed down her long gravel driveway, screaming for help as we pounded on the front door. This neighbor was not as hands on as our nurse mother or the neighbor boy's mother.

At first, she was overwhelmed to see four children in varying stages of bee bites coming through her formal front door. She was more of a city slicker of a mother than most of ours. But once she was able to be calm, her good common sense came through. She assessed the situation rapidly and determined that I was in the most need.

She called to her two older sons who pretty much took the others aside, since they had but a few bee stings. Then she started on me.

When she stopped, she had counted twenty-eight bee stings and had removed not less than five dead bees from my hair. She heated up butter and dabbed all my bee stings with it and had her sons do the same for the others.

With the crisis was under control, she was almost in tears when she called our mothers who were home by then. They dutifully came and got us. Children's emergencies were not her strong suit.

When they heard why we were in the woods, the neighbor's older brother was disciplined. His lie was so convincing to his younger brother, we were all scared when we heard about the potential harm to the kittens. So much so, that our going into the woods to stop him endangered all of us.

When my mother got me home, she immediately put me in a hot baking soda bath and then dabbed a baking soda paste on all my bee bites. Because of my ordeal, I was able to lounge around in my terrycloth robe for a few days, not having to get dressed. Something that was just not done years ago, because we had to get dressed unless we were sick in bed, or it was not a holiday.

The first few days of my recovery, all the neighbor kids and some of their visiting cousins came by to visit me as I sat around in my robe being pampered.

Willful children and guardian angels...

On a lighter note, I guess the tamest memory from those years when I was nine or ten. One summer day I decided to walk down the road in my bathrobe to the boy down the road's house. Something that just was not done back in the 50s. People did not go outside in a bathrobe, not even to get the mail from the mailbox.

But through all this, it was obvious I was a willful child. I thought nothing of it because I had my pajamas on underneath and wore my shoes. But when I got to the boy's yard, the boy's father, who knew me since birth, was puttering with his flowers at the edge of his yard. He saw me in my robe, and plainly told me to go home and get dressed. And I did. He did not even have to raise his voice.

All of our parents watched out for all of us, regardless of whose children we were. It is apparent that the children who grew up on our country road had some guardian angels. If not, I doubt we would be here today. Some of them were the parents in our neighborhood.

Summer Cottages — Grandparents, Parents, Aunts, Uncles and Cousins, Strawberries, and the Country Store

As I have mentioned in "My Hometown" and "Country Living," and "The Toaster," when I was growing up we were surrounded by family and friends who were all connected for generations.

The boy down the road's house was built on land my grandfather sold to a relative of a relative. It was wooden at first. But a fire destroyed it and the replacement house was all brick. It was ahead of its time for a country house back then. One of our dear friends said that the first time she was in their home, she knew it was a city house even though it was far out in the country. This house was next door was my cousins' cottage.

Our cousins' cottage on our road...

My second cousin and her two older brothers were in their late thirties to their late forties when I was between ten and fifteen. They had inherited the cottage from their parents. It looked like a regular home from the outside, but inside it was roughing it for those days. One year when the oldest brother was struggling for work, he and his wife and son, the family decided they would stay in the family cottage year round. They were that kind of close-knit family.

Please, read more about this family and the cottage in "Wintry Days."

My cousin, the sister, never married. She was a beautiful woman, with auburn hair and light-blue eyes. At birth the doctors had a forceps accident that turned her mouth to one side. Her family protected her in her childhood and youth since she had this disfigurement. Never marrying, in some ways, she was somewhat liberated since she had to work to support herself. Inwardly, she acquired a somewhat gutsy outlook on life. Outwardly, her manner was more demure.

She would host annual cottage parties for her coworkers from the national company they all worked for in Buffalo. It was a status thing for her among her coworkers. To them, it was out in the country and so close to our beaches. For them it became a much anticipated annual event for several years. But most of the time, it would just be the families of my first, second and third cousins, their wives and children and my great-aunt Sadie.

Please, read more about being near and in Lake Erie's beaches in "The Lake Effect."

Great-Aunt Sadie...

Aunt Sadie was my Gramma Louisa's sister. My cousin, her niece, called her Salomie to tease her. My aunt did not like her given first name. Most who knew her an entire lifetime thought Sadie was her real name.

When my cousin was almost forty-five, she still continued to hope, even a slim glimmer of hope that marriage would happen. When we were teenagers and we would be around her coworkers at the cottage, my aunt would take us aside each and every time. She reminded us that we were not to discuss my cousin's age with anyone. Not even the family, lest her coworkers who were there might over hear this.

As she put it, "Thinking someone is, or might be, a certain age is one thing, knowing it is another."

Before my aunt and cousin lived together, when my aunt was in her middle to late sixties, Aunt Sadie was the housekeeper for a wealthy, society widower and his sons. Their estate was five miles from our house along Lake Erie's shoreline. She worked there for a couple years until the widower remarried.

At that time, my mother, my uncle and one of my younger aunts were the only ones of her family that far out in the country year-round. We were the furthest out in the country, and somewhat isolated from our large family of aunts, uncles and cousin. Mom enjoyed having one of her favorite aunts within miles. We went to this estate often and had picnics on their lawn.

After that job ended, my aunt fully retired. She did not want to move in with her son and his wife. According to my aunt, her daughter-in-law was a social climber and not someone she was comfortable around in social settings let alone a living arrangement. She and my cousin were companionable. Their moving together seemed a natural progression for both of them.

To the rest of us, my aunt took her role seriously as a dower matronly woman. She was a marshmallow underneath her grumpiness to the children and her terse barely cordial tone to the adults. Kept us all on our toes.

One summer afternoon at the cottage, I was rocking

in a porch chair that really was not a rocker. Suddenly, my aunt said in her usual grumpy voice, "Stop that rocking. It's making me dizzy."

I scoffed at her, continued rocking and said, "My rocking cannot possibly be making you dizzy."

She raised her voice just one more time, without looking at me, and told me to stop. I knew out of respect to stop. Years later when I was in my forties, much younger than she was when this happened, a young child was rocking to the side of me, and it made me dizzy. Life does have a way of making us eat our words.

More summer fun...

Living a short walk from the cottage and being related, and the neighbors on one side of the cottage being dear friends of my cousins and their wives—we all descended on them at whim. Drop-ins were part and parcel of their summers spent at this cottage.

My cousins and their families lived in the Buffalo and Tonawanda, with heat and humidity in the days of no air conditioning in the average home. Many summers when the children were young, the women and children stayed four to eight weeks at a time at the cottage. The men commuted on weekends and took vacation time throughout the summer and stayed at the cottage during those weeks.

Things change...

My cousin, one of the brothers, finally moved to Hamburg from Buffalo after the year in the cottage. As you know from reading "My Hometown," it was the next town from ours and not too far from our road. It was less than fifteen miles from this cottage. Living closer meant his wife, son and he came and went to be with their family for a day at a time, especially when the other brother was there for the weekends all summer.

About the time I was thirteen, the new interstates made it workable to drive into and out of the city on a daily basis. After that, there were summers when the one brother and his family came and stayed all summer. He commuted to work from the country nearly all summer. There were some short times that they would go back and forth between the cottage and their home when their six children matured and had activities they wanted to attend.

Some things do not change and some do...

The oldest brother who had stayed in the cottage for that year eventually moved to Ohio for work and just came home every few years for vacations. But his younger brother, his wife and six children lived close enough in their suburb north of Buffalo that they continued to be devoted to my cousin in her daily life until she passed.

In the summers they made sure she was at the cottage on weekends with them. For thirty years during the winter, they picked her up every Sunday from her home, which was the family home where all three grew up. The winter's day would include church and dinner with their family in their sububan home and then home to her city home. And, whatever vacation time she had from work, she spent with them at the cottage.

My cousin drew us to her like a magnet...

We loved all of our family that came to their cottage. But my cousin was special to all the kids—she had charisma. When we would see the brothers' cars at the cottage, we went to visit. If it was they and their family, we were not as apt to stay for long amounts of time. If their sister was there, she drew all the neighborhood adults and children to the cottage. We all *had* to have time with her.

All this family and neighborhood closeness in a rustic cottage showed me that loved ones and good friends are everything and the place is nothing. Back then, there was no real toilet. Inside there was a chemical kind used for camping. Outside was a rickety outhouse. No running water, it was hauled in from a pump. The wood stove was antique and cooking and washing dishes were chores.

The memory of the family's camaraderie, meals, card games, and sitting on the porch at night watching fire flies in their presence gives me a warm glow to this day. They had unconditional love for each other. They were a treasure to watch and be around.

Strawberry picking cousins and their beach cottage...

Every July and August for many years about the same time our cousins came to the cottage down the road, the "beach cottage cousins" rented a cottage. In June, before this, the beach cottage cousins would come to our house for a long Saturday of picking wild strawberries,

We had acres and acres of wild strawberries behind our house. These acres where our parents had once grown produce had fertile soil. When these cousins came, we were smug country bumpkins. We turned our noses up at their wild strawberries, but they picked away in spite of us. To us those berries were, after all, just there. They were small and it took patient hands to pick enough for anything. Our treat was going to the strawberry farms and picking large strawberries by the quart and eating a quart on the way home.

Regardless of our blathering to them about how insignificant these berries were to us, they were not discouraged. To them they were sweet and succulent berries we ignored. For these cousins it was an annual mother and daughters' event. It led to their making wild strawberry jelly from the fruits of their labor. This activity had untold value to them--priceless.

We would join them in the fields for some of their picking time. Mostly we sat and visited with them eating wild strawberries as they picked theirs to take home. Our baskets were usually empty when we left the fields.

These fields were backed by the big woods mentioned in "My Hometown," Our Tarpaper House," and "The Toaster." The neighborhood children and my sister and I played in it on occasion. But it was dark and intimidating, and quite a distance from our house, even though it was on our property. As I mentioned before, we usually played in the small woods on both sides of our house or in the dryer parts of the woods right behind our house.

In the woods behind our house and Mom's chicken coops, a time or two we kids in a group of about five or six had came across baby rats in their nests. Eeeeoooou.

We knew they were baby rats because they were larger than most mice. Luckily for us, the mother rat was nowhere to be found and we quickly moved on. That discovery discouraged us from that woods as a place to play. Mom agreed with us on our not playing there, too.

On to the beach cottage...

Every summer for many years, our strawberry picking cousins would rent a cottage at Sunset Bay. It was one of their favorite spots. But it was twenty-five miles further south from our road. Their father came out during his summer vacation from work and on weekends until the interstates made it possible for him to occasionally come out midweek and commute back to the city the next morning.

This cousin was one of my mother's favorite nieces and Mom was one of her favorite aunts. And, on my mother's days off, we would go over to the beach cottage a few times a summer and be there all day with them.

Even though we went to the local beach almost every evening with our parents for an hour or two, this was different. A half a day or a whole day at the beach, just hanging out and goofing off was a treat. Time at a beach cottage gave us a chance to sunbathe and collect sea shells. As we became teenagers it gave us the opportunity to do all the boy watching that went with it.

Please, read more about one of these cousins in "Mom's Chickens and Ducks."

The country store...

In between all these summer activities were walks to the general store. It was a mile from our road. The owners were a couple who moved to the country with their five children.

The store walking group included the boy down the

road, the girl across the road, my sister and me. At times we were joined by our strawberry picking cousins who were visiting for the day from the city or their beach cottage, or the children cousins from the cottage. The group varied depending on who was around when the urge to go happened.

We would wheedle loose change from our mothers and the dime Gramma Louisa occasionally gave us. Back then, a dime bought a lot. Money in our pockets and whoever was there at the time went.

We walked four, five or more abreast along the deserted back road that ran parallel with railroad tracks. Something that would be unthinkable in today's world. We ambled along without a care watching the sky and the clouds, talking about absolutely nothing of any importance, just kid stuff.

When we got to the general store, we scrutinized our cash flow and what we wanted. Popsicles, pop, candy or any combination of these depending on what we could afford.

Then we walked home satisfied.

Ah, summers of yesteryear—the excitement, the wonderment, the memories.

My Two Grammas – Gramma Louisa and Gramma Edith

My two grammas were both special in their own ways. We were closer emotionally and geographically to my mother's mother, Gramma Louisa. She lived ten miles from our home. Gramma Louisa would stay with us once or twice a year for a week or so.

There were no scheduled times. It would vary as to just when she would be with any of her children and their families. Since I had eight aunts and one uncle, these short sojourns gave my grandmother quality time with all her children and grandchildren, except the aunt who lived in Florida. And, the aunt she lived with had some time alone with her family. These times gave the rest of us treasured memories.

Please, read more about my aunt in Florida in "Our Family Road Trip."

Gramma Edith, my father's mother, lived in Buffalo, which was thirty miles from our home. It was quite a distance in those days. But every now and then my father, sister and I would make a day of it for a visit with her. But she was only in our home a few times that I recall. Aside from the stereotyping of a mother- and daughter-in-law not getting along, Gramma Edith was a bit eccentric and my mother and she were not close.

Gramma's Easter capes...

When I was between about eight, my Gramma Louisa was visiting us for two weeks just before Easter. Being an accomplished seamstress, she decided to pass the time when my mother was working by making my sister and me capes to wear for Easter Sunday. These were capes we could wear to Sunday school and church all spring and fall, not just for one holiday.

My mother had a fabric stash that Gramma got into and picked light weight gray wool for our new capes. The second or third day at our house she had my mother take all of us to LaClair and Miller's clothing and yard goods store in Angola where Gramma picked out red lining material to go with the wool. The third day into her sewing project, she set about measuring us and making the pattern from scratch, pinning cutting and then she began to sew.

After a couple days the fittings began. She held the pins in his mouth. Something my mother was constantly telling her was dangerous. She admonished her to use her wrist pin cushion. She waved her off and hummed, tucked and folded as she pinned strategic places on each cape. And, we liked the attention of someone fussing over us.

Once, on another sewing occasion when Gramma had straight pins in her mouth, she thought she swallowed one. My mother, the nurse, flew to the cupboard, grabbed a slice of bread and immediately had her eat it. Then she sat down to calm my grandmother and herself.

As they sat there, my grandmother spotted the pin that she thought she has swallowed on the floor near the table leg. She showed it to my mother. Mom did not speak to her the rest of the day and gave her a scowl look for a couple of days.

When Gramma worked on our capes, time after time she would get one shoulder line to meet with her eye of approval but the other would not have a smooth line to match. She took apart the shoulders several times on each cape. After all, she wanted them to look store-bought, not homemade.

Each time she started over, she would say, "Don't tell your mother I'm having this much trouble with these capes."

The three of us would nod in agreement and back to the sewing room she went. We could hear her sputtering and fussing at the end of the sewing room with the door ajar. Finally, the day came when she had conquered the problem and the capes were finished to her satisfaction.

As we modeled them for our mother, Gramma stood back hands clasped, beaming with pride at her labor of love. As Mom slowly turned us around to see every angle and detail of Gramma's work, she touched each cape here and there.

She said she was pleased at how they turned out. Then she turned to Gramma and said, "You're a better seamstress than I am. I could never get those shoulder lines to match."

The three of us burst into laughter.

Gramma Edith's lamb chops...

Whether it was Christmastime or a sunny Saturday afternoon at Gramma Edith's, her home was spotless. She was the fussiest housekeeper I ever knew. Her city flat was immaculate and many who knew her used the old expression, "You could eat off her floors."

She had living room furniture that was used, but looked new. Her old cream-colored lace curtains looked like they had just come from a department store. Her coffee table was covered with knickknacks that gleamed because she cleaned them each week.

Gramma would tell us each and every time, that we should not touch her knickknacks. At times we would hover over them and get close enough that our noses almost touched them. This made her edgy. We did it to get a reaction as children often do. But we never seriously thought of touching them because of our respect for her wishes and her.

At Christmastime she replaced her knickknacks with a small artificial tree with what were probably antique miniature ornaments. And, she reminded us not to touch the tree and the ornaments, just as she had with the knickknacks.

Year round, she had an empty room off her living room that had a turret of windows overlooking her neighborhood. We never quite understood why she did not have furniture in it. But its floors were kept as spotlessly clean as the rest of the floors in the flat.

In her kitchen and back hallway she laid newspaper on her freshly mopped linoleum floors to keep them clean. This never made sense to me because she lived alone. But what did I know as a child?

During our visits to Gramma Edith's when my sister and I were between seven and ten, somewhat to my father's embarrassment, we asked to take a bath. We would not have left the house without being bathed if not that day, then the night before. At the very least, we would have had a sponge bath if a sparse bathtub bath was not possible, since we had to heat our water for the barest minimum of a bath.

Knowing this, she always said yes to our request. A

deep luxurious bath was a treat. My sister and I took turns filling her tub up to our chins with hot water and then languished in it.

Being the fussy person she was, she insisted on scouring the tub with cleanser between each bath. She had her ways. The bather for the second bath got some cleanser grit, no matter how well Gramma rinsed the tub.

Whichever of us was the last to bathe could smell the cooking aroma of the dinner she was fixing us. Her vegetables were from a can, canned corn or canned peas. Our vegetables at home were freshly grown in my parent's garden, canned from their produce, or the produce from local truck farms. But her juicy lamb chops came from a butcher shop and the melt-in-our-mouths mashed potatoes were made from scratch.

She served this fare at her kitchen table. It was covered with a red and white checkered plastic tablecloth. I do not recall a time that anyone ever ate at her formal dining room table. It appeared to be only for show.

Still, at her kitchen table the sun usually shown through her white lace curtains. The food was delicious. The ambiance of this time shared was priceless. We ate every bite of our food, not leaving as much as a crumb.

In the shadows...

As a meaningful aside, my father lived in the shadow of his older brother. My uncle, lived a block from my grandmother. To Dad's family, my sister and I lived in the shadow of my only cousin, an only child. Gramma had daily contact with my uncle's family, if not in person, then by phone. Calling to the city back then was long distance for us.

In retrospect, I am almost certain my uncle helped my grandmother financially in an ongoing way. Knowing my father, I am sure he felt left out that he could not help her in this way. But he did visit her often during the week, because he worked in the city. If he could not visit, we would call her from a city phone before he left for the country. And, he was her gofer since my uncle never owned a car.

Even without a car, my uncle had a family tradition, Just about every Saturday he took my aunt and cousin downtown by bus to shop in the big status department stores of the day. That done, they all went to lunch at the famed and posh Laubie's Old Spain restaurant. My grandmother joined them about once a month and for major holidays and her birthday.

Not really knowing their arrangements, there was a real possibility that my uncle bought expensive gifts for my cousin and put my grandmother's name on them. But even so, Christmas was emotionally draining for us when we visited our uncle's home with our Gramma.

Although, we had a room full of the best possible gifts at home, our cousin would show us her gifts, all overly expensive, designer type toys of the day. They filled the front parlor much as did ours, but it was all for one child. And in the midst of this, there was a very the ultimate doll or toy for my cousin that Gramma gave her.

We were usually undone by these gifts, because we got a dollar in a card for Christmas and a handkerchief in a birthday card. My parents thought this was very unfair, too.

As I said earlier, Gramma Edith and my mother were distant for many reasons other than these gift differences. One of the reasons, unbeknownst to my sister and me, our father had been married before. Divorce was considered a no-no in the 1940 and 50s and was not discussed.

For some reason my grandmother clung to the memory and physical beauty of her first daughter-in-law, even though she liquidated their mutual assets before my father knew it. As I got older, it was apparent to me from things I overheard that my father had loved her dearly but she did not return that love.

My mother was a country girl and stout. But as you know, she was loved by one and all in her family and her community. She was devoted to my father and him to her, they being soul mates.

Back to my story...

Regardless of the frictions and past memories, whenever we were at Gramma's table, all those present and past grinds mattered not. Dad seemed renewed as he enjoyed those leisurely, uninterrupted times with his mother and his children at her table. Time well spent, because he dearly loved his mother and his children.

On the lighter side, my mother was known for her meat dishes like Swedish meatballs and chicken livers to name two. But try as she did, Mom never mastered lamb chops like Gramma Edith.

My Aunt's Dishes and My Uncle's Plums—Land, Trees, White Bibles and Antiques

Whenever I am in a posh department store and see the current fad in dinnerware, I have to smile. These chunky dishes with their cups and saucers, bowls and dessert plates in mix and match colors take me back to a kinder gentler time—the 1950s in my aunt's kitchen and dining room.

As my mother walked into my aunt's kitchen, her step was lighter just being there. And so were mine in the company of these special women.

My aunt was an Italian gourmet cook. My mother, as you know was a gourmet cook, but she sat at her sister-in-law's elbow in wonder. Even if it was something new, Mom would not let anything she cooked or prepared go untried.

Her kitchen and dining room were a cheerful pale canary yellow. Not the subdued beiges or loden greens of my more elitist aunts' homes nor the wallpaper trend of my folksy aunts' kitchens. Over her dining room china buffet was a ceramic silhouette of a man and woman entwined. The woman was in light blue, the man dark blue. They were coordinated in ceramic style, size and some of the mixed colors to her dinnerware and candle holders.

It's not clear to me why I knew that this dinnerware and decor were not well accepted by most of my mother's German English American sisters. I just knew. Children hear things and sense things. If not the actual words, more the tone of how things are said.

My aunt being Catholic, even though many of my mother's sisters converted to Catholicism was not the real friction point. She was Italian. Being people who were raised with a prejudice against Italians, that never set well with my mother's family.

They were not outwardly hostile. But they did not include my aunt and uncle in most of their activities, other than the big family Christmas parties and the family reunions, especially when my grandmother was alive. And in all fairness to my mother's family, this aunt was from a close-knit family of her own. And, my uncle and she did do things with her family more than with his family.

Some added friction between my other aunts and their sisters-in-law may have been her gazelle-like figure and her Latin brown eyes, hair and over all good looks. Not that they were unattractive women, but most of my aunts had robust, matronly figures at early ages. Those who remained trim continuously worked at it. Even though she had many pregnancies, I do not believe she ever had to diet to keep her figure.

My aunts' judgmental comments aside, something just let me know this was a happy person. She enjoyed her different tastes and decors and life choices, even though she was not included by most of my mother's family. But my mother cherished her.

After their son married, my aunt and uncle moved to the upstairs flat in a house they owned. They had lived downstairs in the sunny more spacious flat and rented the upstairs flat out while they were a young with a child to when they were a slightly middle-aged couple with a teenager.

Being in the upper flat evolved when their son married and it was the two of them. They seemed to enjoy the cozy upstairs flat. Then they rented the downstairs to younger families. My one aunt and uncle and two cousins were their first downstairs tenants.

Please, read more about this in "Childhood Antics."

After my aunt's family, who had rented the lower flat for many years bought a house, their son and his family moved into the downstairs flat. This gave my aunt and uncle the closeness of their grandchildren.

Even though my aunt seemed happy overall, moving upstairs was a bit of a down grade for the lady of the house. I have no way of really knowing, but I suspect part of living in a smaller place was easier on her health. More about my aunt's health later in this story.

No matter who lived upstairs or down, both flats had beautiful front porches. I got to enjoy both since I was related to everyone who lived there.

Still, she made it her own. Besides her cheerful kitchen, she had lush brown carpet in her living room. Like her dishes and wall colors, this was not a main stream carpet color. She was once again using home décor that was not all that popular then, but that she wanted surrounding her. But over the years, like the dishes, this carpet has become very fashionable in homes.

In her youth my aunt was a marvel. She lived life in a joyous way. But she had tough times like not being able to have more than one child and her mysterious illness after she was forty-five. Being a devout Catholic, her faith got her through these trials.

Ill health takes over...

A gentle soul, my aunt did not deserve her ill health and lingering death in her late forties. This illness was from something dormant in her health from her youth.

I remember being part of the house sitting for her when she was close to passing. My mother and I would go over on Mom's days off when my uncle was still working, and just be with her. My mother nursed her physical needs.

She had soulful, sad eyes, as she lay there helplessly waiting for the end. As with other family things, I think my uncle was comforted that my mother was able to make my aunt's terminal time better than if she had been in a nursing home.

The land...

Not long after my aunt passed, my uncle donated land in her memory to the Catholic church located in their village. The one side of the church's property was right behind their house. A new two-story priest house was built on the land.

My aunt would have liked that. Of course, even my mother scoffed at this generous gift to the church from her brother. But the land really was boxed in by the houses on my uncle's street and the church's property. There was no access, and this made sense. The land was useless as it sat as part of the unattended back piece of the property. Donating it put it to good use.

The plums...

As children, one thing that was really fun at this house no matter who lived up or downstairs was the back yard. This was the place to be when my uncle's plum trees bore fruit. These plums were delicious. Not the *in* plums of the day at the produce market. Now days, they are very *in* and very expensive.

And, this yard had a huge old barn that was with weathered wood. It was usually empty. We kids always had to go walk in it and snoop around.

My uncle's trees...

Speaking of plums on trees, in the early 1930s, as a youth in President Roosevelt's Conservation Corps, my uncle and a handful of other youths planted thousands of seedling fir trees. They planted these trees along both sides of Versailles Plank Road in my hometown area.

Those trees are now over a hundred feet tall making up wooded areas several acres deep lining both sides of this country road for two miles coming and going. It is a local natural wonder that has given several generations enjoyment, second only to the evergreens in the Adirondacks..

Whenever we drove by these trees we would all say in unison, "There's our uncle's trees."

Things move in a different direction but remain the same...

Some years after my aunt passed, my uncle had a windfall money settlement from a car accident. Formerly a conservative man, he bought a bright red Pontiac LeMans sport coupe. It was an eye catcher and caused comments among his siblings and their spouses.

He was a very generous man and let my sister borrow his sporty car a time or two when she first learned to drive. I was miffed, because he never made such an offer to me. In retrospect, I am sure he did this kindness to my sister, due in part for all the generous and loving things my mother had done for his family and him. And, he thought my sister was a sweet person and good teenager. During the years, I think my uncle gave my mother small amounts of money as a gift every now and then to help her with her finances. She never asked for money and if he did, they kept it between themselves.

The White Bibles...

One Christmas a few years before his windfall, when my sister and I were around thirteen and fourteen, we received the white Bibles with a zipper closing from my uncle. I doubt he initially knew about them or purchased them. He probably gave my mother money to get us something we really wanted. And we really wanted white Bibles. These Bibles were a bit pricey for my mother's pocketbook. He was spontaneous that way.

The memories they shared with us...

My uncle and my mother shared many moments in time through the years. And, we were along for the ride for some of them. In their youth they were rascals together. In their older years they were there for each other.

When they told us stories about their childhood, they would laugh until they had tears in their eyes. They liked remembering over and over, and then telling, the story about my aunts when they slept in a dormitory style bedroom. My uncle had his own room off this open bedroom area. Three of her sisters were married and the youngest was a toddler. She slept downstairs with their parents.

As the story goes, all of the girls would be talking and giggling. At times they would shout something into their brother and he would shout something back to them. Usually, "Go to sleep."

Their father would hear this commotion and bellow up to them, "Do I have to come up there?"

My one aunt, the oldest of the youngest four, barely ten, would say under her breath, "Sure, come on up."

Where upon the others would shush her, so he would not hear her and came upstairs.

Back to the story...

My uncle and my mother being the middle children remained close all their lives.

She always felt his retirement was too early. With time on his hands and somewhat unlimited resources, he was aimless. At sixty-something he married an older woman he met who ran a tavern he frequented. Before his remarriage Mom and most of the family and his son and family knew he was mentally failing.

During his second marriage his mental health continued to decline and there was friction between father and son. It was during this time that my cousin and his family bought their first house and moved out of the lower flat. Regardless of his family turmoil for reasons I do not fully know, his new friends, our family was special to him.

He was widowed again around seventy, and was not far from being institutionalized.

When he was finally infirmed, Mom was semi-retired. At least once a month she drove twenty miles one way to pick him up and bring him to our house for the day. He would sit in a chair on our sun porch, kitchen or living room for the most part oblivious to his surroundings. But she would sew or do house hold things and talk to him. He seemed to connect to her voice and her presence. Then she drove him back. She cried many tears during the drive home but she still considered it a joy to share her time with him.

Mom and the antiques...

My second aunt was childless and when she passed she left all her antiques to my uncle. A year or so later, when his mental health fully failed, their flat was emptied when he went to the nursing home.

At this time his son knew my mother was and antique lover. He told her that she could have total selection of the antiques. They had no sentimental meaning or interest to him. The rest were sold to satisfy the estate.

Among the antiques my mother wanted was a set of eight antique dessert dishes. They had disappeared from the flat. She called one of her older sisters and, yes, she had taken the set. She told this sister that she had first dibs and wanted them all returned to her. Of the eight originals, six were returned. Hmmmm.

My mother had them appraised by her niece, an antique glassware dealer. Each dish was worth $18 in 1970. Mom enjoyed them for several years, but would never use them, nor would she sell them when she needed money.

When my uncle died in 1975, she made sure his son, and his wife were notified about the dishes. She thought it would be nice if my uncle's three grandchildren each had two.

In the meantime during the settlement of my uncle's estate, my mother had a serious stroke and was hospitalized. My cousin and his wife had come to our hometown area to settle some last minute estate details.

My mother had been my uncle's guardian. Even from her hospital bed, Mom insisted that they go to my other cousins and get the dishes. When my cousin and his wife did go to my cousins to please Mom, they said, "We're here for those dishes?"

My cousin, who they were entrusted to, realized their disinterest by their tone, She reasoned that they did not know how many dishes were to be picked up. Being the scamp she is, she reached in the bag and took three out and set them aside. Then she took them the bag with three dishes wrapped in tissue. None the wiser, they left, their duty met.

When we visited my cousin's home during my mother's stroke recovery, she told us what she had done. With that she gave my sister and I each one dish and kept one for herself.

It's been a family chuckle for nearly thirty years now, "If those dessert dishes could talk."

Adventures

As children, regardless of what our family is, rich or poor, big or small, we all have wondrous times as we live among our family and those who become like family.

Mom's Chickens, Cow and Ducks

Childhood Antics—The Bad Seed and the Trike

Kindergarten—the Bus Missed the Stop

Wintry Days—Howdy Doody and Wet Winter Woolens

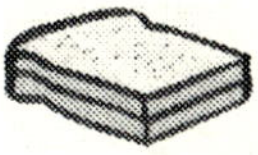

The Sandwich Under the Car

Our Family Road Trip

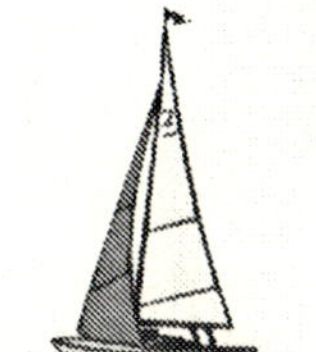

The Lake Effect

Mom's Chickens, Cow and Ducks

In addition to all the accomplished things my mother did, she was a serious and professional capon chicken farmer. But before this, she had a small flock of chickens, and a cow. In between these and her serious chicken farming, she had ducks.

The cow was mean-spirited and often got out of its small pasture. This cow did not like my father. On more than one occasion the cow chased my father. He usually got away, but on one occasion when the cow was over taking him, he took refuge on the roof of the small chicken coup.

He called to my mother who came and calmly walked the cow to its pasture again. My dad would say that that cow was like putty in my mom's hands.

While chickens were one of her best endeavors, for a year or two she added ducks. Eventually, she gave them up. While they were delicious to her and us, they were not all that popular in our area of the country as holiday food. That, and ducks took more work and feed. And unlike chickens, at times ducks became more like pets regardless of the number in the yard.

One summer when the baby ducks were following all the children around, my strawberry picking cousins from the city were visiting. Within an hour or so we found one of the baby ducks dead at the foot of a high tree stump near the duck pens.

The oldest of these cousins, around eight at the time, admitted to putting the duck up on the tree stump. His wings were not developed, and he fell to his death. My mother calmly explained to her that baby ducks and chicks cannot fly. Then she asked her why she put him up there in the first place.

She looked at my mother with innocence and said, "He was acting like he wanted to get up there. So I put him up there."

Over the years, Mom teased her about the duck incident. The gifts she had sent her for many years had a duck theme. My cousin considered it an honor to receive these gifts from one of her favorite great-aunt.

Back to the chickens...

Once Mom decided to be a chicken framer, she poured over chicken catalogs. She ordered just the right breed of chickens for eating and laying eggs. She made sure their coops were clean, the water was pure, and that they had the best feeds. After all, her family was eating these chickens and their eggs

Mom's chickens took up two large coops in our backyard. The area around them was messy. But she liked chicken meat and the fresh brown-shelled eggs. She gave both the chicken and eggs to family and friends and sold them to people she knew.

When I was between the ages of eight and thirteen, she caponized her chickens, making them sexless. This made them plump and meatier for eating. Year round, she stood in our damp basement for hours, at her butcher block table with instruments, operating on these chickens.

She got the desired bird for sale, especially for holiday meals that rivaled the more popular turkeys. Her reputation for succulent, organically fed capons spread far and wide. The phone would ring a month in advance of most holidays. Orders were taken. For each Thanksgiving, Christmas and Easter she would ready her capons, not less than twenty-five birds for scrumptious gourmet delights.

In addition to giving them to family and friends as holiday gifts, and selling them, we had all the chicken meat we wanted for weekly meals and holidays. This was in the years before chicken was a popular meat it is now. Even with all this hard work, and need for the money, her heart was generous to anyone she knew and loved. And they were all honored to be on her gift list.

Childhood Antics – The Bad Seed and the Trike

As you have already read in my family stories, every summer was filled with childhood antics and adventures, most especially summer. In addition to picnics with family and friends, there was Memorial Day marking the beginning of summer, then Fourth of July fireworks and Halloween parties and trick or treating.

Year after year, we had water play in the lake on warm summer evenings. And I can never say this enough about our lying on the grass watching the clouds roll by, napping in a hammock under a shade tree, and drinking home made root beer. Summers well spent.

Please, read more about these times in "The Lake Effect," "Halloween of Days Gone By," and "Wintry Days."

My two cousins, who lived in the next small town to ours in the lower flat at my uncle's house, were from affluence. They were as different as night and day. The boy was five years older than his sister. Trustworthy, reliable, the good one.

The girl was akin to the bad seed. As a child her parents dressed her in what we considered Sunday school clothes to play and her thick blonde hair was braided. Still, this picture of innocence always made us feel like she was contemplating setting fire to my uncle's barn in the backyard.

Once as we sat at my aunt's kitchen table eating peanut butter and jelly sandwiches, I (the oldest of the youngest cousins), looked out the window to see my aunt's car rolling down the driveway backwards. The bad seed was standing behind the wheel. We all ran after the car like the characters in a Laurel and Hardy movie.

The car came to a sudden stop when it rolled into a ditch rather than a nearby ravine. Its front wheels were up in the air as it sat on its trunk.

In the panic of the moment, the speculation of the car rolling down the ravine went wild. The reality was there was a forest of trees at the end of the road that the car would have surely hit and stopped. Before that, the houses along the way would have been another barrier to the car even rolling into the woods.

My two cousins, the boy down the road, the girl across the road, and us...

Whenever we were all playing at our house, the added children in this mix of cousins were the boy down the road and the girl across the road. The boy was, a good boy whose family like ours was prudent with their resources.

When my sister and I were about six and seven, we were playing outside with our cousins on a warm summer day. The boy down the road had his first new tricycle. He was beaming with pride as he showed it to us and we were happy for him.

As we stood there admiring his treasure, my older cousin lifted the trike from our circle of admiration and threw it in the small creek next to our house. In shock and disbelief we--my sister, the boy, the neighbor girl, even the bad seed, and I--all wailed like the kids in the Charlie Brown comic strip.

My mother and aunt came to see what had happened.

Naturally, my aunt instructed her son to retrieve the trike and apologize which he did. But what happened next was beyond our childhood expectations.

She spanked my cousin as she dragged him toward our house with the intention of doing this for the full length of our gravel driveway. My mother stopped her from any further spanking and dragging. Our thirst for revenge waned and turned to sympathy—we did not want him punished that much.

Ah children, ah memories.

Kindergarten – the Bus Missed the Stop

When our daughter was in Kindergarten, she took the wrong bus. By the time the bus driver discovered her sitting in the back of his bus, he was at the end of the line. He asked her name. Then he called the school and told them he was bringing her back to school.

Before the school called our house, her bus went passed and she did not get off. I began to worry. We lived near the school and she should have been one of the first off the bus. I called the school with my concern. They assured me she was not there waiting and must have boarded another bus, a common occurrence with kindergarten children.

They assured me they would check the school and contact all the bus drivers. The phone rang a long half hour later. The school explained what had happened. They said they would be driving her home after the bus returned her to the school.

I watched and waited for the car to arrive. When it pulled into our driveway, I rushed out the door.

The transportation superintendent drove her home. I could see the top of her head in the backseat of the car behind him. As I walked to the care, she had one of her loud pouts on her face. As he opened the door to let her out, he was very apologetic to me for the mix-up.

She pushed passed him, leaped into my arms and buried her head in my shoulder.

As I thanked him for bringing her home, she raised her head up long enough to glare at him, but said nothing. He left. As we walked into the house, she began to cry and told me she was so scared she would never get home again.

Life repeats itself...

As this happened, I felt her fear and sense of abandonment. It took me back to my kindergarten days.

My mother worked part-time then. Occasionally, my younger sister and I would stay with a neighbor. When school was out, the neighbor, the neighbor's youngest child and my sister would pick me up at the bus stop a mile from her house.

On a few occasions the neighbor did not have her car and could not pick me up at my bus stop. The few times this happened, my mother asked another friend if I could stay at her house for a few hours until she could pick me up.

The friend's son was in my class. We did not know each other very well. But I knew him enough to ride home with him on the bus. In all, I probably went to their house three or four times in Kindergarten.

He had a birthmark on his forehead. This was new to me. But after a while, I did not notice it. He seemed to not be aware of it either. His large family did not seem to notice it.

And he did not seem dashed by it. He was a high spirited boy, a bit daring do.

One of the times I went home with him, he got up on a stool to get into the freezer of the refrigerator to get us ice cream. Added to the possibility that we were probably not supposed to have ice cream, I was worried he might fall.

He seemed to have done this before and all went well. No falls and we were not scolded. It seemed his family routinely kept ice cream in their freezer. We did not have ice cream in our freezer unless it was there for a special occasion.

One of the times I was to go home with him, he was out sick. But I knew I was to get on his bus. And I did. The problem arose when I did not know exactly where to tell the bus driver to stop. I had only been there a time or two before at this point in time.

I stepped to the front of the bus and told the driver I was to be left at his house.

The driver slowed some, but did not stop. By the time the driver believed me, we were nearly an eighth of a mile passed the stop.

This would not happen in today's world, and should not have happened then, but it did. He just stopped the bus and let me off that far past the house and told me I would have to walk back there.

I was scared.

But I walked back toward my friend's house. Half way there, a man in a car went by me. He was a young father and knew who my family was. He had seen me a time or two with my mother.

He thought, *That looks like Vera's girl. What is she doing here alone on this road so far from home?*

Concerned, he turned around and drove back to where I was. As he pulled alongside me, I was nearly trembling with fear that I would be snatched.

He rolled down his window and asked me if I was Vera's daughter.

In my fright, I did not realize he must know me because he knew my mother's name. But I did not know him. I would not answer him.

I kept walking.

He asked me where I was going. I would not answer.

He asked me if I needed a ride somewhere. I would not answer. Finally, he decided to follow me until he could decide what to do for me.

I kept walking as fast as I could. It seemed to be an eternity until I saw my friend's driveway and got to their door. When my friend's mother opened the door and let me in, I was relieved. She noticed I was scared. I told her about the man following me. She knew him.

She waved to him and he to her. Then he left.

When I was in my early thirties, I re-met this man and his wife. Both good people that eventually I had known personally when I was older. I had forgotten this incident until he retold it to me. Until then, I did not know it had been he who followed me to safety. I thanked him for being so caring and watching out for me.

It was then I realized, all those years later, I had a guardian angel that day. And, that God is with us at all times through those he sends our way.

Wintry Days — Howdy Doody and Wet Winter Woolens

In the winter whenever there are days upon days of snow, we stay inside with a snowfall state of mind. Cozy by the fireplace or television, we drink hot drinks. At times, I think back to the winters of my childhood, a time when we were without a television in every home.

We have come along way through television--to the moon and back--all televised worldwide. Since 2000, we are on our way to Mars and beyond with television giving us a look-see with every adventure.

In the 1950s, few homes had a television. Difficult to believe now, with American homes having 2.5 televisions. So, it is nearly impossible to imagine sharing a television with the neighbors.

The television programs we did have gave us a meager offering of shows. But what was available had an impact on our lives and our neighborhoods. Televised shows were usually from noon to the late news between ten and eleven o'clock at night. There were exceptions like the "Today Show" and "Arthur Godfrey." The most popular shows in the evening were variety shows like "The Texaco Hour" with Milton Berle. The drama shows were "Hallmark Hall of Fame" and "I Remember Mama." During the afternoon children's shows began about three to four. Howdy Doody was the most popular. At Christmas time the local Santa Claus shows were a must see.

About 1953, we were one of the first families to have a television because my uncle, an aerospace engineer, dabbled in television repair. It was a black and white table model with a six-inch screen and a huge case. To bring the screen to a "seeable" size, approximately twelve inches, it had a giant magnified glass that sat in front of it.

Eventually, we progressed to a floor model with a fifteen inch screen. In the early 1960s, our first portable with a twenty-one-inch screen with its own stand was a big leap for us. In between our television acquisitions, as each neighbor bought a newer larger model, all the children in the neighborhood shared their sets by open invitations to watch children's programs.

Year-round we would not miss Howdy Doody, Monday through Friday, we could watch it at home. But it was more fun to go to the house with the latest larger screen TV, usually all of nineteen inches. We would watch television together all afternoon after school and go home just in time for supper.

During our Western New York winters, before the days of water resistant materials, woolen winter clothes were all we had. Once wet, they were not worn again until they were fully dried. This took hours of hanging near a heat source.

In spite of this, we would trudge through the snow to our friend's house, peel off our wet layers of clothes in the cellar and hang them to dry as much as possible in the furnace room while we watched afternoon television. Then we walked the short distance home in damp woolens.

It was worth any discomfort, because we were driven, afternoon television waited. It was ours for the taking. And, once home we could warm up.

One winter's day we trudged through the snow to the

boy down the road's house. As usual, we went into their cellar and took off our wet winter woolens and hung them up to dry some while we watched television. Or, so we thought.

Just as we finished hanging up our wet winter clothes, the boy's mother opened the kitchen door to the basement to get some canned goods for dinner. When she saw us, she said she did not know we were there. Then she told us their television was on the fritz and her son was next door with our cousin.

Slowly we put on our wet woolens. The cold wetness made it an unpleasant process accompanied with some groaning and wincing on our part. Once we succeeded, we went next door.

Our cousin's mother cautiously let us in. This was the cousins who were making due in the family's summer cottage year round. They were not set up for winter, let alone company with all these wet woolen clothes.

The mother was a city gal and her son was an only child. She was not accustomed to having a group of children in to watch television. This was an inconvenience for her just before dinner. But she was polite and we were invited in, after all we were relatives. And in part, out of pity for our wet clothes. To our surprise she made all of us hot chocolate.

Once Howdy Doody was over, we were shooooed off to our respective homes. After being warmed, our clothes seemed even more cold and wet. But we were buoyed up by our shared time with childhood chums. And we had an hour with Howdy Doody, Buffalo Bob Smith, Clarabell the Clown, Princess Summer Fall Winter Spring and the peanut gallery.

The Sandwich Under the Car

When we were growing up, the back fields behind our house had a large woods at the end of our

property. Occasionally, our parents would walk with us to the edge of the woods. From there we could faintly see other houses off in the distance. Their properties backed up to ours.

Please, read more about the woods that divided our properties in "My Hometown," "Country Living" and "Summer Cottages."

One of those houses belonged to my mother's acquaintance. She was a sister-in-law to one of Mom's best friends. This made her like family to us. And, she had a small farm and raised fruits, vegetable and chickens like my mother did. This gave them several interests in common.

But that is where their similarities ended. This lady, had a very unusual way of housekeeping, even for back then and out in the country. By that, I mean that things that would normally be kept in the garage, the shed, or the barn, were routinely found in her house, as were her animals. We had a dog and cat occasionally, but she had dogs and cats inside and out. Lots of them.

But my mother looked past that because they were friends.

And, since truth is stranger than fiction, I should

mention as fate would have it, this neighbor lady and my mother eventually had apartments across the hall from each other when they retired. My mother enjoyed her apartment being a mix between semiformal and casual. On occasion, she would have some small gardening items in her kitchen because space was tight. Still, she always shook her head at her neighbor's apartment being just as back woodsy as her house once was.

Back to my story...

One summer's day, we went to visit this neighbor. As usual, my mother and her friend began gabbing and looking at the farm produce and the chickens.

About lunch time she invited us to stay and eat with her. My mother said yes we would stay. My sister and I looked at each other in disbelief. We were very skeptical. Very.

On more than one occasion, we had overhead our parents talking about what a good person this neighbor was. How she had a kind heart. But neither of them would want to eat at her house.

We tried to coax my mother to leave. But she insisted we stay and eat with her friend. So we stayed out in the yard playing and talking sister things until they brought us the food.

Hamburgers on white bread.

I was concerned. Even back then our parents preferred we eat whole wheat bread. My mother saw my apprehension. But she told us it would be all right this one time, and that we should to go ahead and eat the sandwiches.

The burger was not as well cooked as I would have liked, but I ate it. My sister would not eat hers. It was not cooked enough she told me. I looked at hers and it was nearly raw.

What to do? Not thinking this through, I put the sandwich under the car.

When my mother came out, we left, her friend waving us off. As we reached the end of the long dusty driveway, we told our mother what we had done. As she drove down the road, she sternly told us to come and show her the food next time. She would make sure it was right. She made us promise to never throw food away again.

Then she laughed one of her deep down funny laughs. My sister and I looked at each other. We were puzzled at the laughing.

"With any luck one of her dogs ate it before it was even noticed," she said as she continued to laugh.

Mom always had a way of making it better. We continued on home with a warm breeze on our faces and our loving mother at our side.

And, it became a family joke for a while when we ate away from home, often at picnics. We were told not to throw any food under the car. Then the three of us would laugh together at our private joke.

Our Family Road Trip

In 1958, when I was in the eighth grade we went to Florida. It was Easter time during spring break. Our parents packed us into our family's 1956 Chevy station wagon and headed south.

Before this trip, we had driven around upstate New York as far east as Rochester for the lilac festival. And on special occasions we went to nearby Pennsylvania and the border areas of Canada near Niagara Falls.

This was different. It was a serious road trip.

Imagine a trip then compared to now. No air conditioning, six people and our luggage packed into the station wagon with us. We became five because my mother offered to take an elderly friend of hers with us. This traveler became a problem along the way, but more about our happy adventures and that later.

Number six was a middle aged woman from our town that my mother slightly knew. She was riding with us to get to Florida to be with her sick mother who had retired there. We did get relief from extreme crowding when we dropped this gal off at her parent's home. But the trip to, through and back from the Sunshine State was prickly.

Added to this eclectic group, there were no interstates, two lane US highways at best with a few divided highways. Every road went through a city or town. Occasionally, there was a progressive city with a business by-pass route. Credit cards did not exist and we paid cash for everything. No 800 numbered reservations, we took our chances with motel vacancies each night.

Disneyland had just begun in California. Epcot was not even a glimmer in Disney's eye. There was no Walmart, Kmart, and few if any national and regional food chains. Kentucky Fried Chicken was a chain then but just in the south.

You get the picture. Still, back then we knew of no future conveniences. To us, for the time and place, it was a wondrous trip.

Each state was scenic...

We drove down through Maryland and Virginia, passing the eastern edge of the famed Blue Ridge Mountains. We found it interesting that Maryland had such a small land mass. Dad said, "If you blink your eyes you will miss this part of Maryland."

The Carolinas and Georgia were something we did not expect. We were shocked at the slum cabins in South Carolina and in awe of the hanging moss on the trees of Georgia. Once in Florida, we dropped our one-way passenger with her family and continued to drive down the east coast to Miami visiting family and friends along the way.

Vero Beach was our first stop at the home of one of Mom's nursing friends. We went to the ocean as soon as our luggage was in the guest bedrooms. Afterward we were covered with salt and had to take showers. This was not how it was in our hometown in Lake Erie's fresh water.

Please, read more about out summer swimming adventures in "The Lake Effect."

Somewhere between this stop and Miami we stopped

to visit and stay with a second or third cousin. Over the years she repeatedly asked our family to visit her if we were ever in Florida. She did not have children and did not seem to care to have my sister and me there overnight.

The expense of a motel was out of the question for our travel budget. So we all made the best of a not so pleasant situation which gave my mother and her cousin the visit they wanted.

From there we went to Daytona Beach. We were in awe of it as my Dad drove our car on that famed beach. We had our first southern fried chicken there. Not long after this, Kentucky Fried Chicken began to go around the country for everyone.

From Daytona, we went to Cypress Gardens and saw their water show. But we were waylaid by the park's personnel and to Mom's disappointment we did not see the lush gardens. Then we went to Orlando's well known Boch Tower. This was the only tourist draw of that time there.

Getting to Orlando was scenic and safe in the day time. At night, it was an entirely different situation with highways that had no shoulders. Added to that, the roads were like driving on ice, with snakes that crawled out of the swamps onto the highway.

Dad had to use his snow skid techniques to keep us safely on the road and not have our car land in a swamp. We were all very quiet, scared and praying, as he drove us to civilization.

Once the east coast of Florida, and Miami and Orlando were in our rear view mirror, we went to the gulf coast. Our primary visit was to be with my aunt, uncle and cousins in Tampa. Time permitting we were to fit in a short visit with some friends from our hometown in New Port Richey.

Visits with my aunt, uncle, cousins and good friends...

When we were a couple blocks from my aunt's house, my parents decided to stop at a grocery store for some food stuffs for our motel later than night. A motel was necessary since we knew my aunt's small house barely accommodated her family of six.

My sister and I asked to walk the few blocks to my aunt's house while my parents were in the store. Something we could do safely back then.

She was expecting us that day driving up in a car. At the house we saw her in the back yard hanging up laundry. We walked up to her and began chatting with her as if we lived in the neighborhood. She started to visit with us over her shoulder and then suddenly realized fully who we were. She stopped doing the laundry and the hugs and kisses began. Shortly after this, my parents and our traveling companion drove up to the house.

We visited my aunt and my cousins as each one returned home from school. My uncle came in just before dinner. But my aunt had not added to her dinner preparations knowing we were there all afternoon. After all, we did not just arrive at the dinner hour. So we did not have dinner with them since they said they had not expected us that day. Maybe, maybe not.

Really? If memory serves they had spaghetti. Now that I am a mother, I am puzzled at this, because who cannot add to spaghetti. But they gave us ice tea while we sat in the living room waiting for them to finish their dinner.

Why would we just sit there? My mother wanted more time to see her sister. And, we wanted that for her.

We took the high road and said,, "No problem we would eat when we got to our motel."

At our motel we ate in the adjoining restaurant. Then,

tummy's full, we sat out on the lawn furniture enjoying tropical breezes as we thought of the colder northern temperatures were had left.

The next day we were headed to New Port Richey. We had a wonderful day long visit with our friends. They had a lovely lunch ready for us on their screened patio. After a lazy afternoon visit, and discussions about alligators in their yard a time or two, we picked cumquats in the sun. At the end of the afternoon they offered us dinner and we accepted.

They asked us to spend the night in their very large home along the water's edge. We probably could have stayed indefinitely with our friends but time was not on our side. Dad and Mom had to get back home for work. And, Mom wanted one more day with her sister. So we headed back to the Tampa motel we stayed at the night before. We wanted to be close to my aunt's house for a long day's visit before we drove north.

My mother was driving us to back Tampa. It was just about dark. Being on unfamiliar roads she missed our turn. Finally, everyone in the car noticed it did not seem to take this long to drive this route in the morning. As we all looked around, we seemed to be out away from any cities. To our surprise as we thought we were arriving in Tampa we saw the city sign, "Welcome to St Petersburg."

Being green tourists, we turned around and went back to Tampa. Had we given it any thought, we could have stayed in St. Pete overnight and seen that city as we left in the morning on our way to back to Tampa.

Some odd and not so enjoyable things about our trip...

Back then, fresh squeezed orange juice was sold at

rough-hewn roadside stands. This was before frozen juices. Until that trip, we had had canned juices or fresh squeezed with store bought, barely ripened oranges when they were on sale.

Being northerners, as we entered Florida, we began to consume large amounts of this fresh orange juice. By the third day we were all getting a rash. Nurse Mom realized we were not drinking enough water but we were drinking too much OJ!

At each beach, my sister and I searched for the elusive star fish. Alas, we had to settle for the store bought kind just before we headed north.

While searching for star fish, we had a close call. At our second beach on the edge of Miami, we gathered transparent sacks of blue liquid into piles on the beach. Only to find out they were a dangerous variety of stingrays. These stingrays were missing their tentacles or we would have been seriously injured, paralyzed or even blinded if the sacks broke and the liquid had gotten into our eyes.

Before we leave this family memory...

Our traveling companion began to be a concern when she wanted to smoke in the car. Without air conditioning with car windows open, her cigarettes blew sparks back to the clothes and luggage in the station wagon's cargo area. That meant no smoking in the car.

But for her to agree to that, we stopped for her cigarette breaks in addition to our rest stops. Something my parents were not wanting to do, neither being smokers. These breaks took our daylight for driving and sightseeing. With coaxing, she agreed to smoke at rest stops. This meant she took longer in the ladies rooms to have her cigarettes. While it continued to be aggravating to us, it was a concession we all had to make. All though at times, my Dad would just say to her, we could not take time at every rest stop for a cigarette. That was that.

Being Catholic, we had to stop for her to go to church. While we regularly attended church and Sunday school, this was not something we planned to do on our "once in a lifetime vacation." She insisted. Irritation was high when we had to stop twice for her church attendance since this was not mentioned as a necessity when the trip was being planned.

Catholic churches were not that plentiful in the south then. For her first church stop, we drove around Winchester, Virginia for a good hour to find a church for her. Her only church in Florida was in St. Augustine. We waited outside the church and talked about Ponce de Leon and his discovery of the "fountain of youth" and marveled at the wonders of the flora.

Prickly things aside...

This trip was something special for a small town family. It was exciting to be in these places, even with all the unknowns, struggles in our travels, and dangers for tourists on the beaches. It was a trip none of us ever forgot.

The Lake Effect

No visit to my hometown and the memories of my youth would be complete without a visit to Lake Erie's shoreline. For years much of Western New York is equated with ice, snow, and blizzards.

As each winter begins and ends each year in that part of the country, the words "lake effect" come to mind. All my life those words have been the reason for bad weather in the surrounding region. Usually, it is linked by local and national weather reporters year-round to inclement weather.

As a person who grew up four miles from the beaches, who has traveled to far reaching parts the world and back very few waterscapes have exceeded our beaches. As a child living in the Southtowns, at times Lake Erie and its beaches were taken for granted. How could we know before television took over our lives and took us to global places, that there was any other type of geographic community?

This gave us time to concentrate on our own locale, undisturbed. And concentrate we did. We swam all summer and played on the beach at the many lakeside parks. Our parents took us swimming every evening at Evans Town Park. This was a rich time of no cares, no worries. The sounds of "Mom, Dad, watch this" to every water play still echo in my mind.

Up to the age of ten, it baffled me as to how every living person was not in the water with us. I knew there would never be a day in my life that I would not be in the water in the summer, "no matter what." Ah, yes, the projections of youth.

While children still swim and play at the beaches of the lake's shore, all it takes for me to mellow is to sit by the water on warm sand, listen to the water swish and lap, deeply breathe the moist air, read, listen to music, or just sit and soak it all in. Now that I am grown, It is my sand and water therapy whenever I can be there in the summertime.

In recent year, some have referred to the lake's shoreline as Buffalo's "Riviera." In all honesty, that comparison was never part of my growing up years. And, living away from the area as an adult, I had not heard that. But after reflecting on the many beaches in my travels, it does ring true.

The shoreline is picturesque. It is a place to walk, wave at friends, watch the sunsets, swim, play, sun ourselves, meditate, enjoy the camaraderie of other "lake people," or just sit and BE.

One September I sat at Sturgeon Point, my hometown marina and watched the breathtaking sight before me. The lake and the sky were the same color blue. There was just enough haze that the lake and sky merged. I lamented at not having a camera. Then my realization was that no film or camera combination could record this pristine moment. So I sat there and soaked it into my memory to draw on at any moment, any where in the world.

Translucent blue. Calm waters. Table top smooth. Rough waters. Like a mirror. Aqua mist and waves. Tranquility and blueness.

This is what Lake Erie and the surrounding waterways mean to me. This was and is my *lake effect*.

Special Times

Love comes from above and finds us through our family and the village that is our extended family.

Lazy Hazy Days of Summer

Bible School and the Palomino Horse

Hiding out in the Choir

The Violin

The Hawthorn Tree

Mom's Barely Soup

The Lazy, Hazy Days of Summer

Every summer when the air is warm, some might say hot and still, but not sticky and there is a pleasant breeze every few minutes, the breeze surrounds me. It takes me back to the summers of my youth in Western New York.

Those summer days we would walk under shade trees from one activity to another. Or, sit under trees at Bible school for hours listening to Bible stories and singing hymns, waiting for the end of each day's session just for cool aid and cookies.

Please, read more about Bible School in "Bible School and the Palomino Horse."

As you know, we had many family picnics and beach days and evenings. And there was always the annual family reunion. My mother's family was close and my aunts and uncle would gather with children and grandchildren, sons- and daughters-in-law with the matriarch, our grandmother. And the younger generation would eat and eat and eat, while the adults would eat and drink beer from a keg.

They were not really drinkers the rest of the year. So a warm afternoon and the endless beer brought on some astounding effects. By early evening they would hold the family meeting, no one but my aunts and my uncle, if he was there, could sit in on this council.

As they circled their wagons to begin the meeting on

the patio or porch of the house the reunion was at that year, they were obviously "feeling no pain."

One aunt lived in Florida. The same aunt you read about in "Our Family Road Trip." It was their tradition to make a group call to her from the reunion, sharing the expense. After this call, they would get silly, even weepy, and suggest they charter a plane and have the next reunion in Florida. As they sobered up this plan was always scuttled. The closest they ever came to this extravagant of a reunion plan was chartering a bus. This idea was discussed for a good week after that reunion until it was forgotten.

Another tradition, each aunt had a specialty dish that she made each year. We ooohed and aahhhed over all the tasty dishes and deserts. No shortcuts were taken. Fast foods had not even been thought of yet.

One aunt was known for her baked beans. As a young child I just ate some of everything my plate would hold, even seconds and thirds from those large food tables.

As I approached my teens, my taste buds became more discerning. About this time, I noticed that my aunt's baked beans were dry and tasteless. Could this be a fluke?

When I asked my mother if she noticed how dry the baked beans were, she shushed me and nodded in agreement. Then she told me in a hushed voice that it was her sister's *thing* to do and no one had the heart to tell her how dry they always were.

Aha, a time of realization for me. One that taught me to see passed the actual food and take in the ambiance of these gatherings, the whole as it were.

Please, read more about these family summers in "Country Living," "Summer Cottages," "The Lake Effect," "Childhood Antics" and "Bible School and Palominos Horses."

Ah yes, the lazy, hazy days of summer as the Nat King Cole song said it so well.

Bible School and the Palomino Horse

As a child, I was obsessed with Palomino horses. It may have had something to do with the Roy Rogers television show. Trigger was a golden Palomino. And the truth be known, I seldom if ever went around horses. But I had pictures of them around my bedroom and constantly talked to my parents about wanting a horse of my own.

My Palomino horse years were also my Bible school years. Bible school was the highlight of our summers when I was growing up. Our bible school ran two weeks and our teachers were dedicated volunteers.

We opened our days with a morning hymn sing and then went to our classes. Many times in the days before air conditioning we would go outside to sit under shade trees. We memorized Bible verses word for word, one each day, and made crafts. And I am sure the subject of Palomino horses was discussed during craft time when there was no particular bible work being done.

My favorite craft from those years was a copper planter we made for our parents. The teacher who taught us how to do this was an accomplished artist in many mediums in her own right.

During Sunday school year round, this talented teacher drew figures from the Bible with pastel chalks while she told us a Bible story. As the story unfolded, the people from the Bible were there for us to see. As a child and an adult, I have been to some collectively creative Sunday schools, but never to one with that much talent in one person.

As our Bible school teacher she put in the extra effort, even though her personal life was fraught with serious hardships and struggles. But she never mentioned them. She was a decidedly cheerful person at all times.

When I finished Bible school that year, I had memorized all ten Bible verses word for word. The school gave us a certificate at the parents' night program. And that was that, nothing more was expected by me.

About two weeks after the end of Bible School, there was a knock on our door.

When I went to the door, to my surprise, my Bible School teacher was standing on our front porch. She had two shoe boxes in her hands.

She said that she had two students who had written the bible verses perfectly and wanted to give each of us something special. Being a ceramic artist, she had two of the most beautiful ceramic horses to offer us in those boxes. Since I was the first student she came to, I had first pick.

As I looked at the shoe boxes and then back at her face, she had a twinkle in her eyes. There, to my surprise, was a golden Palomino ceramic horse. I chose it. And with that she was on her way to the next student's home.

For years that Palomino horse rearing up on its hind legs was a treasure among my childhood keepsakes. Not for what I had done to get it, but for the special heartfelt joy my teacher had for me. And in a small way it filled my need for *my* horse.

When I was a teenager, for some reason I cannot recall, it fell to the floor of my bedroom and broke. I was undone. I cried. Carefully, I put my broken horse in a shoe box and was determined to glue it back together.

Over the years that followed, my expertise did not lend itself to restoring the horse. When I offered to buy another one, my teacher was older and not able to do ceramics any longer. Finally, as I was moving my things to my first home after my wedding, the broken Palomino was put to rest, and sadly tossed in the trash.

Over the years, this teacher and I would connect, if only for a few minutes at church when I was visiting my hometown. As an adult I noticed that she was a bit gruff and probably always was. Not something a child would notice.

She did not seem to garner the town's appreciation as much as I thought she should. Back in the 50s and 60s, many volunteers like my mother and this teacher were not honored as they do now days. Community service was just done without fanfare. Even so, she was someone I wanted to be like.

Some years later after a long illness, when this community humanitarian and dedicated teacher was near her passing, I wrote a thank you tribute to her and mailed it to her. Her sons said they read it to her and she was pleased. That same tribute was published in our local paper. It was long overdue that my hometown knew in black and white just how special she was.

She knew the hearts of the children she taught and was a true shepherd to her flock.

Hiding Out in the Choir

When I was around eleven, our Sunday school had try outs for the youth choir. My sister and I eagerly went.

For years our church and youth choir was directed by a great gal, who was like family. She and my aunts had gone to school together and she and one of my aunts remained lifelong friends.

As we sang different songs, it was apparent that I could not carry a tune to the degree required to sing in a choir. The choir director came to me and said as gently as she could, that I had a strong voice. But it would need training to sing in a choir. This youth choir only met before Sunday school briefly and she did not have time for voice training.

While I took this critique well, on the surface, deep down I was disappointed. After all, the other kids who tried out sang in the choir including my sister. It was the thing to do and the place to be.

But I had heard my dad say that neither my mother, nor I, could "carry a tune in a bucket." But as a young teen, I had been optimistic until it was a definite no.

A few years later, when I was enrolling in a new high school in a different school district from where we lived, the guidance councilor suggested I sign up for the school chorus. He told my mother and me that singing in this chorus meant an extra half credit each year toward graduation, an easy two credits.

When he made this chorus suggestion, I told him about my Sunday school experience, but he waived me off. He said something like, "They'll never find an off-key voice in over thirty voices."

Mom and I looked at each other and shrugged. He signed me up.

The first two weeks of choir went well. But one day, the choir director said she wanted each section of the choir to stop singing at her direction. The other sections were to keep singing until she got to them. One by one, section by section, she stopped the singing until she was in my section.

At the end of class she asked two of us to come in after school to see her. We did.

Then on dry throats, as if a wet one would have helped me, she had each of us sing "America the Beautiful." The other gal sang in her church choir but had a cold that week. She was told to stay. Then she turned to me.

When I sang, it was pitiful. She asked me if I knew I was off-key. I admitted I could not carry a tune. She asked me why I signed up for chorus. I told here it was the guidance counselor's suggestion. He said no one would find me in all those voices.

She said, "Well, you go back and tell him, I found you in all those voices."

Years later, I was able to tell both of these fine choir directors these stories. One I told when we attended church while we lived briefly back in our hometown area. The other, I told at a high school alumni dinner. My high school chorus director looked better at seventy-something than when I last saw her my senior year. She was dressed in a beautiful, long, blue dress. She sparkled. Sadly, she passed the following year after that meeting.

My Sunday school choir director is still with us. She always looks cheerful and still is contributing to our church and our hometown.

Each felt sympathetic thinking back to how this must have impacted me. As I said to each of them, you should not be concerned. They each did what they had to do.

Now days and for many years, I sing in church and around the house and to any Neil Diamond song. I remember singing in Sunday school regardless. But after that high school fiasco I did not sing in church for many years. Did not even pay any attention to unfamiliar hymns but hummed along with more familiar hymns.

A few years after high school, I lived on my own away from my hometown. Living in Louisiana, a completely different culture from my northern roots, I attended church with new friends.

The first Sunday in a new church they offered to share their hymnals. They looked puzzled when I declined. When they stopped singing, they asked me why I did not sing. I said, "I cannot carry a tune."

With that said, as the service progressed I was looking around the church and daydreaming. When the responsive reading began, one of my friends nudged me and said, "You can read, can't you?"

The Violin

When I was in the fourth grade, our music teacher held the annual assembly to pitch music lessons to us. The lessons eventually would lead to our playing in the junior and senior high school bands or orchestras.

After the assembly, I wanted to play the violin.

My parents were less than enthused when I showed them the permission papers to sign for the lessons. And the contract papers to rent the violin, after all the lessons were free. But neither of them wanted to sign a year-long contract to rent an instrument that might sit in the hall closet for half the school year.

Ahhhh, they knew me all to well. Still I insisted. I *had* to take violin lessons.

My mother said she would sign for the lessons if we could borrow my uncle's violin. She called my uncle and he was willing to loan us his violin.

When we got the violin, it needed all its strings. Something we had not anticipated but by this time my mother had signed the papers and we were committed.

It was $20 for the strings. A lot of money back then.

As it turned out, there was another girl taking lessons with me. I knew of her. We were both considered tomboys by our classmates.

In the beginning of the lessons, I practiced and enjoyed playing the violin. But as the first half of the school year progressed, I stopped practicing. I felt I could play the lessons in the class without practice. The teacher disagreed.

Not long into the second half of the school year, I began to forget my violin. At first the teacher had me play some of my lessons on the other girl's violin. But soon she would let me watch and listen. By spring, I had stopped taking the lessons. The violin, in its case, sat in the hall closet.

The following fall, my mother returned the violin to my uncle. He in turn gave it to his daughter. My cousin was a talented interior decorator in each and every home she had.

The violin was placed on the wall of her family room surrounded by artificial flowers. And for many years after that, my mother would grumble about the violin that cost her so much money to become a wall hanging.

But one thing came from my interest in the violin. It was my appreciation for a good violin player. Two who come to mind are the famed Jack Benny and Florian Zabach.

For many years Florian broke ground in television with a weekly show. He was a music celebrity of that time, before Liberace.

When I was seventeen, Florian was playing at Kleinhan's Music Hall. Mom and I went to hear him play. Truth be known, Mom was humoring me to go. But once there, she was impressed with his music.

To this day, it gives me a warm feeling to have been there with my mother. This concert was one of our special mother and daughter memories.

The Hawthorn Tree

Spring and summer reminds me of our yard and my mom's blossoming trees. Any flowering tree caught her eye as we drove though the countryside. She would point out various blooming trees and bushes but the dogwood in bloom always took her breath away.

From time to time she would pull to the side of the road to snip a dogwood branch to take home and enjoy. At that time it was illegal to cut or disturb dogwood trees in the wild. She would shush us when we mentioned it.

Most of our horticultural delights were given to us from other gardeners or came on the wind. But every now and then Mom would buy some bulbs, a lilac bush, rhododendron bush, a wisteria vine, and a hawthorn tree or two.

Please, read more my mother's green thumb in "My Hometown" and "Easter Time"

Yes, the hawthorn trees. One was a deep fuchsia bloom on the high side of our yard that could be seen from our picture window. The other, a pale pink, Mom planted off to the side of our driveway. It was a flat area my parents had filled over the years with rocks, dirt and eventually top soil that angled down to our small brook. Out of the way she thought. And for many years, it was babied and watered and left undisturbed.

For our northern part of the country, it was an unusual

pastel pink color. So much so, each year several friends and neighbors would comment on how pretty the almost translucent blooms were.

The year I learned to drive was not a good year for that tree. We had two cars and one was a somewhat light 1956 Chevy station wagon and easy to stop. The other, a big heavy 1953 Packard sedan nearly took both feet on the brake to stop it. Especially if you were young and inexperienced as I was.

One evening, my dad and I did an errand in the Packard. It was about dusk when we returned. I turned into the driveway a bit fast, and to my surprise, we had company. Their car was in my anticipated parking spot. Not wanting to hit that car and crash both cars into the garage, my youthful split second thinking saw the open lawn with the hawthorn tree. Yes, I stopped before going over the edge of the knoll. But no, not in time to save the tree.

Mom shed tears over that tree, like losing a friend. I shrugged it off, glad that I had saved the day. But when I was older, and had my own gardens with special plants and shrubs I finally could feel my mother's sadness at losing her hawthorn tree.

The wonders and beauty of nature feed the soul. My family had those everyday riches so many take for granted. Nature gives so freely. My mother always knew that.

Mom's Barley Soup

Recently, we discovered a "dive in face first and never look back" chocolate cake. It is not famous, but it should be. We discovered it in a small BBQ place, not five miles from our house. This cake, that is only a dollar a piece, is moist with frosting that could be eaten by the spoon. And, you would not care to count the calories.

To our surprise we discovered that the gal who bakes this delicious cake does not even like to bake. We asked her if this was a special recipe.

"Oh, no," she said," I got the frosting recipe off the cocoa box." Then she added, "All though, I do get some ingredients imported."

Aha. There is a special recipe. Hers.

This brought to mind my mother's recipes. When my mother had passed and the details of her memorial service were in place, my sister and I were reminiscing. We began to discuss her special dishes.

We relived the cozy winter evenings when the aroma of Mom's cooking wafted thought the house. We ooohhed and aaahhed over the memories of several of her culinary delights, some even decadent. As I mentioned earlier in this book, until we were about seven and eight, she had also grown many of the vegetables and fruits she cooked or prepared.

She would pour boiling water over her vine ripened

tomatoes and peel them. This made them melt in our mouths with mayonnaise on them. And, until we were eleven or twelve, she broasted her capon chickens.

Each of us had favorites. But we both were experiencing nirvana when we remembered her German potato salad, breaded chicken livers, superb tossed salads that were different every time, watercress salad with hot bacon dressing, and melt in your mouth potato pancakes.

Mom even made fruit-flavored ice tea that rival the commercial brands of today. Her secret ingredient was her homegrown mint leaves and maraschino cherry juice. And, she made ice cubes out of ice tea with these ingredients in them.

All those dishes could probably be replicated, even though we would only come close to hers. But we doubted we could make her barley soup. A soup, her sisters never made, perhaps out of respect for her recipe. As you know, her family was like that, giving the due to the cook whose dish was theirs.

We could *taste* her foods, as we thought back to her humming around our kitchen, creating as she went, just as great cooks are known to do. As we continued to reminisce, mouths watering, we wondered who would have her barley soup recipe.

At the time of the memorial service, since we lived out of state, we stayed with one of my mother's dearest friends. When the memorial service was over and the well wishers had left, she and I sat quietly having some tea. As we discussed some shared memories, the conversation turned to the family's wish for the barely soup recipe.

"You're a good friend," I said. "And you both swapped recipes over the years. Is there any chance you would have Mom's recipe for barley soup?"

Without saying a word, she quietly stood up and went to the kitchen and unceremoniously returned with a box of barley. She sat it down on the table in front of me. For a few seconds I was baffled.

Finally, looking at the box of barley, I said, "Yes, the barley soup recipe, do you know what it is?"

Without fanfare, she picked up the box, held it toward the window light next to us and pointed to the recipe on the side of the box.

"That's it," she said. "The recipe is on the side of the box."

The mystery was solved!

And, we knowingly laughed out loud because, as anyone knows, a written recipe is just words on paper. It comes alive to the delight the taste buds because a cook who is a true artist adds a pinch of this and a dash of that. Mom was that kind of artist.

Celebrations

Holidays and celebrations are the milestones that we look to for reassurance that our lives have meaning.

Birthday Parties and the Red Umbrella

Easter Time—Flowers, Egg Coloring and Fruit in the Basket

Halloween of Days Gone By

Grampa's Christmas Desk

Mom's Christmas Gifts

Birthday Parties and the Red Umbrella

Our birthday parties were a neighborhood event. When my mother planned a birthday party for us, she invited every child in the neighborhood regardless of age. They all came except those who had a cold or were out of town at the time.

One year my sister lay on her bed moaning and groaning the day before her birthday party. Mom felt her throat, as nurse and doctors do. My sister had developed swollen glands. Mom would not want any children to be exposed to anything, just in case it was contagious. She had to call all the children and cancel the party.

As I overhead her making the calls, this day, it was difficult to tell who was more disappointed, my mother or my sister.

My most memorable childhood birthday party was my ninth. Every child in the neighborhood was there save a few who could not come. My gifts were the usual and were not even remembered more than a year or two, except *the* red umbrella from my parents.

This was my gift request from them, still they surprised me with the umbrella. I opened it in the house and had all my birthday guests join me under it. Except for one younger boy who did not like umbrellas or there was no room with all the children crunching closely together.

My mother intervened and even he was included in the umbrella caper. Then she made me put it down, because it was bad luck to open an umbrella in the house. And in a party group that size the metal tips of the umbrella could have hurt one of us.

After the party was over and we were putting my gifts away, my parents cautioned me not to open my umbrella on a really windy day. According to them, it could cause the umbrella to flip inside out and break. Made sense. I made the usual mental notes of what they told me.

But two short weeks later, they must have left my memory. It was a cold and icy March day. My mother took my sister and me with her to an Orchard Park chicken farm to look at a breed of chickens that she was interested in ordering for her capon business.

She said she would only be a moment. We were to stay in the car. We were warmly dressed in winter woolens, so this was not a problem.

Time must have gotten away from her and dragged on for us. My sister was the content one and sat there with no problem. I, on the other hand, with my red umbrella got out of the car.

As I was shutting the door, my sister held the door ajar and told me not to get out of the car. But I assured her it was just going to be a walk in the driveway close to the car. I would get in before our mother came back. I shut the door.

Deciding to open the umbrella, no sooner was it open and the wind grabbed it out of my hands. It did not break it. But it did blow it upside down on its tip with such force it raced down the long slick icy driveway. It was amazing to me at how it blew with great speed toward the road. I could not run after it without falling.

My mind went racing. If that umbrella went into the

road and was crushed by a passing car or truck, my parents would be upset.

Slowly, I pursued it. Suddenly, the wind stopped and it stopped. I was able to over take it, grab it and close it.

My heart was pounding from this close call. Slipping and sliding on the driveway, I got in the car and calmed myself before my mother came back. My sister just sat there with a smirky smile. Neither of us said a word.

I learned my lesson. Don't open an umbrella in the wind. And do what your parents tell you to do.

Easter Time—Flowers, Egg Coloring and Fruit in the Basket

Easter time was a special time for our family, more so than being a national and religious holiday. It meant baskets and baskets of goodies, colored eggs and wearing flowers to church. And, it meant flowers inside and outside of our home.

Nothing lit up Mom's face like a spring flower. As her long awaited spring flowers began to bloom, she knew the beginning of our yard's bountiful blooms lay ahead.

This blooming season included Myrtle in our woods, violets woven in our grass, the white blossoms of our locust trees, lavender and white lilacs, pink and burgundy hawthorn trees, and white rhododendron bushes. Roses were mixed in with the ivy next to the house and down the hill. Under Mom's care, we had climbing lavender wisteria over the old pump and pachysandra edged the lawn near our front door. The adjudga cushioned our walk around the pool, the mixed-colored porttulacca along the side porch, and the mint under the picture window for ice tea were some of her delights.

At Easter time, Mom's spring display was in the twenty-foot rock garden alongside our gravel driveway. In it she planted every daffodil, narcissus, hyacinth, tulip, iris and crocus she could fit in. It was breathtaking in full bloom, so much so that family and friends asked to have their picture taken with it, even in the days of black and white photography

Many years we would get carnation corsages for church. Years later we bought orchids. As a family we favored red and white carnations. When we could, we would take daffodils right from our garden and pin them on our Easter coats. In recent years, in the absence of that lovely garden, we each wear a single rose.

For years, on Easter Sunday afternoon, Mom would take us to the Buffalo Botanical Gardens. The long line to get in was no deterrent. As children, we would wait, not always patiently to queue up to the entrance.

One Easter season after we moved to Kansas, Mom, my son and I went to the famed Belle Plain outdoor gardens. Acres and acres of daffodils, jonquils, narcissus, tulips. She was overcome with the joy of such a display. According to her, these gardens were rivaled only by the spring gardens in Holland.

She was not one to have her picture taken, not even beside our spring garden. But in these gardens she posed gladly to have a fixed memory of her time among the blooms.

Every Easter, amidst the spring flowers, the Easter Bunny ritual was a given. Over the years, the Easter baskets of our childhood evolved into fruit baskets of our teens.

When my son was a young child, we made a conscious decision to put fruit and hard-boiled eggs in his baskets. And, as long as the Easter Bunny was part of his life, for excitement we would hide his colored eggs around the house for him to find. He was constantly amazed that the bunny would hide colored eggs around the house when he left them all in his basket the night before.

We enjoyed coloring eggs, but not as much as Mom, who had a child's at heart for any holiday. When we were younger, Dad even participated in the production. This meant buying just the right egg coloring supplies. As teenagers, my sister and I carried on the egg coloring more for Mom than for us.

When my mom came to visit my family over the years at Easter time, she set aside time to color eggs with her grandchildren. And when she was not with them, wanted pictures taken of them coloring eggs.

Her many gourmet foods brought a festive air to any holiday. But at Easter time, her pickled eggs were gobbled up by everyone who had the chance. Her special recipe, which I now aspire to every spring, had the usual ingredients with a twist. She put beet juice in the pickling mix to color them a deep pink. They melted in our mouths, like no other hard-boiled egg could.

Baskets were another one of Mom's loves. She did not limit them to Easter, but had them every where in our house year-round and gave them as gifts. She carried her crocheting and knitting in them to and from work. Many's the morning when she arrived home from the night shift as a nurse, with an orange in her basket among her yarn. The orange was part of her work meal. She brought it home to eat it later. She was just that way.

One year when our son was nearly five, we were visiting Mom for an extended summer stay. After work, she came in with her usual basket. Our son spotted the orange among her crocheting in her basket.

"Oh, look, the Easter Bunny left Gramma an orange."

Halloween of Days Gone By

Each fall as the trees change colors, autumn breezes swirl their leaves to the ground. The rustle of leaves still takes me back to a time when my mother was consumed by the thrill of planning our annual Halloween party. Celebrations were her passion.

As you have read in "Our Tarpaper House," our house was built by my parents as they could afford to do it. For the most part it was austere, but we had a walkout basement and garage second to none, perfect for Halloween parties.

The preparations were a family event. These preparations took on a life of their own as we made costumes, bought soft skinned Macintosh apples for dunking, and hung black and orange crate paper, and paper skeletons and black cats from the basement beams. Our carved pumpkins lit by candles were set by the entrance to greet ghosts, goblins and our guests.. And we tirelessly gathered bushels of leaves from our special woods at the side of the house and dumped them on the cement floor until it was ankle-deep for effect.

Oh! Those rustling leaves!

Year after year, I was dressed in an evening gown from our old dress up trunk with a mask and fake fingernails. I did my best to hide my identity and was always amazed when guests arrived and knew who I was. Children!

My sister usually wore the costume she wore for her dance recital in the summer of that same year. One year when my sister was in elementary school, her tap dance class were monkeys. My sister was not happy to wear a costume where she had a long tail hitting people and things behind her.

That tail. Only a dance teacher would think of it and not the sewing abilities and hassle it would take to make it. When my mother made that dance costume, she sputtered as she had to sew the costume's tail and then turn it inside out. Stuffing it was not easy either.

Some years we wore our costumes to school for our classroom parties. The one I remember the most was my sister's witch costume. When my sister was in fourth or fifth grade my mother decided she would wear not be wearing a dance costume to the Halloween parties.

Mom decided my sister would be a witch. Mom could make the black loose fitting costume to go over her clothes for school, trick or treating and our party. And, she made the witch's hat from heavy black construction paper. And, as always, being creative and ahead of her time, she decided to snarl my sister's blonde hair to look witchy.

As we rode the school bus, one of our older girl friends noticed the snarled hair. She told my sister it looked like here hair was not combed and the other children would laugh at her. My sister, as you know from other family stories in this book, was a shy child, even in the upper grades. She just sat in her seat and said nothing.

With that, the girl proceeded to gently comb out every snarl. I tried to stop this. I told her our mother had planned to have her hair that way. But my objections were waved aside and the blonde hair was combed to the smoothness of corn silk.

Back home for our party, the witch with the snarled hair and the glamorous princess greeted guests to the rustle of leaves on the floor and the scent of warm cinnamon cider. It always surprised us that we were recognized when we opened the door for our guests. Kids.

At each of these parties, we bobbed for soft skinned McIntosh apples, sang, played games, and tried to pretend for one short evening we were someone else.

The day after each party we swept up those wondrous fall leaves and hauled them back to the woods to become one with nature under the winter's snow.

As I revisit these memories, I think of all the children who came to our parties over the years—children from our former neighborhood (all were included) and the special school chums we invited—and wonder about their memories of those times.

From time to time, as an adult who does not live in my hometown but visits often, I see these "children" and we hug a knowing hug from childhood shared.

Ah Halloween, what memories do you have?

Grampa's Christmas Desk

No one ever really knows what makes a gift become a memory for a lifetime. The Christmas I was ten, a large seven-drawer desk was delivered to our house. My parents told us it was from Grampa Aber. It was unfinished, but my dad, as you know, was proficient in painting and refinishing, finished it in a beautiful natural wood look.

It began with a large delivery truck that took up our driveway as it backed into it. The unloading process was an awesome event for us. The box it was shipped in was so big, they used a hoist to take it off the truck lowering it to the driveway.

Our family had a real cherry wood desk that my mother considered hers. It had been with her since before we were born. It was high quality, high-dollar desk that was a fixture that we took for granted. But this desk was new.

We sat at that desk for years. My sister and I had our sides. From year to year, we took turns using the center drawer. When I left home and married, my sister painted the desk blue to modernize it to go with the bedroom walls.

After we both had been married, my mother loaned the desk to my cousin and her children enjoyed the desk for many years. Finally, when we moved back home during a family transition, our children enjoyed it in their younger years and then again in their teens.

But back to the gift...

Getting such a large gift from him was a surprise to us. Grampa was not very close to our family. He was an enigma to me. As a child I did not see him much.

As I learned when I was older, he was a special person. My grandmother and he had mutually separated when my father was in his early twenties. He had faithfully supported my grandmother, even after his retirement by personal integrity without a court order, to honor their agreement.

Regardless of the steady financial arrangements, this separation caused extreme anger toward Grampa with both my uncle and my father and among themselves. Even though they knew my grandmother only married their father to get out of the house.

In the late 1890s, paternal approval was necessary for a girl to marry, or she remained an old maid. My grandfather was the only young man her father supervised on the railroad and approved to date his daughter.

They moved to Easton, Pennsylvania, where he worked. It is a border town in Pennsylvania not far from their Washington, New Jersey hometown. From there he followed the railroad man's job for companies, first to Akron, Ohio, then to Bethlehem Steel in Buffalo, New York. He eventually retired from there and lived in South Buffalo.

When I was in the Easton area for about a year in my thirties, I did walk on the same ground where my grandparents grew up and married, and my other ancestors lived their lives. I found the street where my father played as a child. And, I was able to re-meet a second cousin, who had met me when I was a child.

Back to Grampa...

When my sister and I were around seven and eight, we would stop to visit Grampa. He and my father were cordial and we sat on the front porch where he lived. I remembered being dressed in Sunday school clothes.

One of these visits seems like it was yesterday. Grampa was unshaven. He wanted us to give him a kiss good-bye. We barely knew him and we were both repulsed by his gruff looks. We both shook our heads "no."

Undaunted, he offered us a quarter each if he could have a kiss on the cheek. I, being the oldest and the brave one, agreed, and kissed him on the cheek. He gave me a quarter.

But my sister was steadfast in her decision. She was shy and could not be bought. I think he gave her a hug against her wishes, but did not force her to kiss him and gave her the quarter anyway.

But when it came to that Christmas desk, the truth be known, my grandfather probably gave my father some money for a nice Christmas gift for us. He would do things like that occasionally, perhaps in hopes that he could draw some closeness to his son. But that was not meant to be.

Many years passed after the desk arrived, and not much visiting went on between my father and his father, or Grampa and us. But, for that time and place, it gave Grampa some bittersweet enjoyment of what time we had together. And we felt he got some joy from knowing his gift was the desk.

Finally during one of our moves, we noticed the desk was barely holding together. We said our farewells and gave it a final rest. As wooden desks of that vintage go, it probably lasted more than most of its day. And, we were well served by it.

Mom's Christmas Gifts

When it came to Christmas, my mother delighted with the innocence of a child all her life. She would plan for it all year, join Christmas clubs and begin her purchases in July. When we were married, she would (at great personal sacrifice) send generous amounts of money to us and even buy us Christmas clubs to ensure our adult Christmases. And most years she would save her money all year to fly to where we were.

Our house was decorated inside and out the nth degree. One year Mom took slide pictures from the outside with a simple Brownie camera. They came out crisp and clear. So much so, we have a copy hanging on the wall of our home to this day. As we look at that picture, we feel as if we are standing outside our house, looking at the festive lighting and watching the festivities inside from our snow-covered lawn.

Our tree was a picture—balanced lighting and ornaments and each piece of tinsel was individually hung. Each year my father began to detail his train collection from November to mid-December to insure perfection under the tree.

Our Christmas bounty literally covered half the living room. Santa always left us matching dolls and one year they had matching authentic baby buggies. Our stockings were stuffed with fruits, nuts, special chocolates, dime store goods and treasured collectables. Many times it took all morning to get to the bottom of our stockings.

Shaking the boxes...

As children, my sister was the patient one. While I would shake boxes and listen intently to the noise the content made. As the years went by, I could neatly unwrap and rewrap presents to see what I was getting.

When I was around ten, my mother's employer gave her an extravagantly wrapped gift from an elegant downtown department store. Beaming with pride and filled with excitement, she placed it in the center of our gifts under the tree.

Each day for several weeks I would shake the box to see if I could guess what it was. To me, the mystery was unbearable. My sister would stand with me until the shaking was over and I would shrug and we would both walk away and go about our day.

On Christmas morning, my mother, who usually waited for us to open all our big presents and start on our stockings went right to her gift. As she opened it, she ooohed and aaahed to see it was a ceramic bird. Something her employer knew she would like but never buy for herself, even though she was a bird lover and lifelong bird watcher.

When she had it unwrapped, she held it up to admire only to discover the beak was broken!

She was upset that her employer would give her a broken gift. When I saw the disappointed look on her face, I confessed to shaking the box several times. To try and guess what it was. My sister nodded in agreement, saying she saw me do it. And I admitted that I had probably broken it.

My father suggested she tell her employer that it was broken. No but she said she had "half a mind " to call the department store and complain about their gift wrapping department. But she never did. She glued the beak on the bird as best she could and put it on her collectables shelf.

Years later while Christmas shopping in the Panama Canal Zone, I saw a high quality ceramic rooster for $7 at our base exchange. The price was substantially less than in the department stores of the time. Immediately, I thought of Mom, not only a bird lover and watcher but someone who enjoyed the sound of a rooster crowing in the morning. I bought the rooster for her Christmas gift that year.

Back to my gift...

After carefully wrapping it, I rushed to the US post office on base to mail it in time for Mom to have the joy of opening it on Christmas day.

Even with spongy type packing, it did not meet postal regulations for breakable contents. Repacking would have caused an oversized package that would put it into the boat mail category. This would take too long.

Dashed and discouraged, I wrote and told her about the rooster. And about my attempt to mail it. All was not lost, because we each realized she would get the rooster when we saw each other in person.

Once we returned to this country, we spent most Christmases together. Her trips would to be with us, were her continued gift each holiday season to us. Even after she retired, she worked part-time private duty cases to pay for her airfare to where we were. A few times near the end of her times with us, she would come at Thanksgiving and return home just before New Years.

The first Christmas we were back in this country, at the end of her visit with us, she was able to put the rooster in her suitcase and very carefully get it back to her home in Western New York from Kansas. She placed it in a special place she had made ready for it in her new fireplace room which was her gift to herself that year.

As adults with our own families, our visits home were usually in the summer when the children were out of school. On one of these visits about ten years after I had given Mom the rooster, I noticed the tail had been broken and glued. Immediately, I asked her what had happened.

As she sat in her favorite chair knitting, she calmly said, without looking up from her craft, that her grand-nephew had accidentally broken it. He was riding his hot wheels in the living room when she babysat him.

A ride-a-toy in the living room? This from a mother who would not let us run in the basement. She saw my bewildered look and threw her head back as she laughed her special laugh. A laugh I inherited that my husband calls my dirty little laugh.

As we sat there that sunny day, enjoying each other's presence, she put down her knitting needles and looked out her picture window. Finally, she said with an impish smile, "I remember a little girl who broke the beak off a ceramic bird. After all, material things are temporary."

Printed in the United States
27200LVS00001B/436-483